In Love with A
Southside Nigga

Written By,

HYDIEA

Copyright

ACKNOWLEDGEMENT

First and foremost I would like to thank God for giving me the strength to complete this book, as well as my friends and family for all the support that was given to me in order to make this happen.

To my mother, Ratanya. Thank you for supporting for me and having my back through everything.

Thank you Racquel Williams for giving me the chance to get my book out there.

Thank you to Christine Davis, for rocking me. I appreciate you.

Shout out to Kevin, Damika , Niecy, Keke , Alesha and David. I appreciate y'all for rocking with me.

Chapter 1

Mica

Back to Today

It's been 48 hours and Mike has been drinking nonstop. I'm scared for my life because I know what comes after, so I go in the room, lock the door and prepare myself for what is about to come.

"Mica, MICAAAAAA! Girl, you hear me. Get yo ass out here and get me another beer!" I sat silently until he knocked at the door. "Bae, open the door. Come on, open it." I was thinking to myself, *If I open this door, I might not see tomorrow.* Then I had this bright idea. *Girl, make him promise not to hit you.*

Dumb? I know.

"Mike baby, promise not to hit me," I begged.

"Baby, I'm sorry, just let me in. I won't touch you. I love you, I promise".

So, my stupid ass opened the door. He walked in, hit me right in my face and head butted the hell out of me. I was screaming, "YOU PROMISED!" Nowadays, if you don't have your word, you don't have nothing. Your word holds a lot of weight when it comes to people trusting you. Especially for a man. If you can't be a man of your word, you not shit!

He replied, "I promised I wouldn't hit you." He began to choke me all the way to the floor then kicked me over and repeatedly while saying, " I love you. I love you. You better not leave me." I was coughing up blood when he finally stopped. He turned me over and started punching me.

"God, just take me now, PLEASE" I screamed.

I couldn't fathom the fact that he was beating me this bad. I'm nothing but 140 pounds and 5 feet tall.

"Oh, you want God? Guess what? He can't save you!" He ripped my shirt, ripped my shorts, pulled my panties to the side and began to have his way with me.

Each stroke felt like my life was leaving me. Each stroke felt like I was dying and every slap to the face brought me back to life. I remember passing out and woke up to what I thought was warm water, but he was pissing on me. Once he finished, he looked down at me and said, "You belong to me and don't you ever forget that. Now get up and go clean yourself up.".

I couldn't move. I didn't understand. I was lost, I was confused, I was stuck with no one, and I couldn't leave because I loved him.

This is clearly not the first time Mike has put his hands on me and quite frankly, I'm getting sick of it. I wash his clothes, cook his meals, fuck him in whatever position he loves, give him amazing head, and I cater to him like he's the only person on this earth, and in return, he treats me like shit. How could this even be possible? How can God send someone your way, make you fall so deep in love, and let them abuse and use you? I've heard about females going back to men that beat on them, and I used to call them silly and dumb. But look at me now. I'm the dumb one. Running back to him faster than I could blink. We don't have kids and we have nothing going on that I couldn't leave. What was I doing?

While I was in the shower, I cried my eyes out. I was crying so long that I sat down in the shower letting water ruin my new Brazilian hair. I didn't give a shit now. I wanted to get out the shower, grab a knife and stab the fuck out of him. I finally got out the shower and there Mike was, laying on the bed asleep like he just got home from a hard day of work. This was the perfect time to fuck him up. I went to the closet and grabbed his shoe box where he kept his gun. I stood there with the gun in my hand for 15 minutes. Finally, I tapped him on his foot with the gun.

"GET YOUR BITCH ASS UP!"

He woke up in shock and scared. This scared look on his face was so amusing. I was now in control. Just like he held my life in his hands, I now held his life in mine.

He started stuttering, "Baby look, you don't have to do this. I swear I won't hit you anymore."

I said, "Yeah, you swore the last time but instead, you choked me and pissed on me like I was garbage, you bitch ass nigga! You think I believe anything that comes out your lying ass mouth? For SEVEN years I been holding you down. I should be happy with a family and a loving ass husband. Instead, I'm stuck with a woman beater." I started laughing. "Yo ass really sitting there sweating. Baby, you scared of death? You don't like this feeling, do you?" He didn't say shit to me. just looked at me dumb founded. "BITCH ANSWER ME! Did you ever fucking love me?"

"Of course, I loved you, Mica."

"Then why you treat me the way you do? After seven years… why?"

"Baby, I don't know how to answer that, but I do know I'm so sorry for treating you like that.".

Mike has never been sorry about shit, so I knew he was lying. *He just saying anything to get me to put this gun down.* Knowing that, I cried more. Mike will never love me like I love him. I had to live with that.

"You know what? The only way I'm going to get away from you is if I kill you."

"No baby! Please chill out. For real, don't do this."

I pulled the trigger. Nothing came out the gun, no bullets, no loud pops. Mike grabbed the gun out of my hands when he realized with a smirk on his face. At that moment, he realized I was going to shoot his ass for real. He hit me in my face with the gun and pistol whipped me until I passed out.

Mike put me to sleep for 3 hours. I finally woke up with blood dripping from my head. This was crazy. Yes Mike hits me, but he has never made me bleed like this. I woke up confused as fuck. I began looking around the room for him, but he was nowhere to be found. I stumbled to the kitchen and he wasn't there either. In my head, I felt like he just left me for dead. How could he? I went to my purse and grabbed a cigarette. I promised myself I would stop smoking, but he is the reason I still do. When me and Mike first got together when I was in high school, I was smoking. Not because I thought it was cute nor cool, I just had a lot of shit I was dealing with. Back then I was being tossed from foster home to foster home, being raped, abused, everything bad thing you could think of happening to a teenager; I lived it. For the past week now, I kept a pack in my purse for moments like this. It helped me calm my nerves a little and take my mind off everything that was swimming around in it. I was halfway through my smokes when my house phone began to ring. *"Who could it possibly be?"* I started to think.

"Hello?"

"Girl, where the fuck you at? You told me you were going to meet me at the mall at 2. Its 4-o clock, bitch."

I looked at the time and she was right. Me and Jas been friends since grade school. I told her almost everything, and she always knew when something was wrong with me. Me and that girl were like Tia and Tamera even though we looked nothing alike. I'm dark skin, 5 feet tall, long hair, and slim thick. Jas is light skinned, 5'9 and super thick. She didn't start developing her body until we got into high school. Her and I became the best of friends fighting over a boy; we literally got into a fist fight. Afterwards, we walked home together because she lived a few houses down from me and ever since, we have been attached to one another.

"Damn. I'm sorry. Something came up."

"Why you sound like you in pain?" Jas asked with her voice getting louder.

"Don't worry about it. I'm good, girl," I said, lying straight through my teeth.

"Yeah, okay. That nigga better not be over there smacking you upside your head. I don't know why you won't let my brother beat his ass. You know Wes has had a thing for you since we were freshmen in high school girl. That boy would take a bullet for you."

"Girl, I said I'm fine. I'll call you back in a little bit," I said before hanging up.

Wes was Jas brother; I never took him or anything he ever said serious. He was always a huge ladies' man. When we were in high school, all the thot whores wanted him, which made me want him less. He was too much of a show off, and I was not into all that attention. The attention them girls were giving him, I wouldn't be caught dead giving. And besides that, I didn't have that kind of time on my hands. Plus, at the time, I was head over hills for Mike. I was 14 and Mike was 18 and a senior in high school my freshman year. Mike had dreads down his back, chocolate, tatted up, brown eyes that would make your pussy wet, 6 feet tall, and muscular. Mike was the star player on the boys' basketball team. However, once he got his scholarships taken away, everything turned bad, and he changed so drastically. The school would have random times that they had the drug dogs come in and smell around. Well, on this day, Mike had a few bags of weed in his locker, and quicker than you knew it, everything was going downhill. It was like when he was told he was not going to be playing basketball for the rest of his life, he turned into this evil ass person.

Wes, on the other end, was everything that any girl could dream of and more. He was light skin with hazel eyes and tall. He always treated me with respect, even if he was a little bit of a whore. A few years back, I seen Wes and told him about how angry Mike gets. He told me that whenever I'm ready, he would handle him. Mike was a hood nigga, but Wes was THAT NIGGA in the hood. Niggas never crossed him because they knew he would really go there, and that's what I feared. I didn't want to send Wes Mike's way and Wes ends up killing him; that's the kind of nigga Wes is. He controls practically the whole south side of Chicago. Niggas moved when he said moved. We all know that kind of control brings problems like murder and a bunch of other bullshit I don't got time for. As if there wasn't enough violence in Chicago, why would I add to the murder rate?

Finally, as I'm putting my phone on the charger after talking with Jas, Mike returns in the house. He bought me peroxide, band aids and gauze. I know this nigga didn't just beat the shit out of me, now in my face trying to play nurse? He has some muthafuckin nerve.

I looked at him, and he said, "Hey, clean yourself up, baby girl", as he was handing me the bag with all the first aid shit. I didn't even say anything back to him. I went to the bathroom and did as he said because only Lord knows how far he would go with this. Thank God I'm brown skinned. After I clean myself up, I won't look as bad and it won't be as noticeable. Mike been calling me his chocolate beauty since we were kids, and yet he chooses to fuck my face and body up, leaving me with scars for the rest of my life. Once my face heals, it won't be noticeable at all with makeup.

While I was in the bathroom, I decided to hop in the shower. Mike walked in right after I finished washing up and got in with me. He grabbed me by my face and said,

"Baby, I love you, and I don't mean to hurt you."

Then he started kissing me. I started crying because I have heard this shit a million times. It all began to sound like a scratched record. The best apology is changed behavior, and Mike not gone change for nobody, not even himself. As he was kissing me, he opened my legs and slowly rubbed my pussy. The tears that were just in my eyes were caused by pain. The tears now are caused by pain and pleasure. Mike always knew how to have his way with me and how to make my body feel good. As mad as I was at him, sex with Mike is always amazing. His fingers felt so good teasing my clit. He knew the perfect way to do it. While his fingers were in my pussy, he began to kiss my neck and lick my ear lobe. I leaned my head farther on his chest while grabbing the back of his head and pulling his dreads. Mike started breathing in my ear. I gasped for air.

"You like that, don't you, baby?"

"Yes," I moaned.

He pinned me against the shower wall then bent down and ate my soul out of my pussy. Mike knows I'm not the kind of girl that likes you to just focus on my clit; I like my entire pussy eaten. I started riding his face. His tongue was deep inside my pussy while his nose was rubbing against my clit. He must have needed some air because I was ready to drown him in all my pussy fluids. He took small breaks to kiss my thighs. I started moaning real loud because I was about to cum.

He yelled, "You better not cum until I tell you to!"

Him saying that almost made me cum harder, but I held it in. I loved the aggressiveness about Mike during sex. If only he could learn to keep his hands to himself outside of the bedroom. He got up and turned me around, then inserted his 9-inch dick in my pussy.

He moaned, "Damn, baby. I love this pussy." I was so wet. Although we were in the shower, I could still feel my thick juices sliding down my legs. He grabbed both my hands, held them above my head and started pounding me harder and harder.

Mike must have known he fucked up with pistol whipping me because this is the first time in forever that he came inside of me. He let off that load, moaning so loud.

"I want you to have my baby."

Now, I said yes, but I do not need to be having a baby with him. That would be the worst decision I could ever make. I can barely keep myself safe. How in the hell am I going to keep a child safe?

I thought after he came he was done, but he wasn't. He pushed me down and put his dick in my mouth. I was shocked, but he was still rock hard. He fucked my mouth for a good two minutes, stood me back up and inserted it in me again.

"Now cum," he said. "Baby, cum for me. Cum all over my dick."

A few strokes in and I did exactly what he said. I let all my juices out on his dick, screaming louder than Kirk Franklin and the Choir, "I'm Cumming!" As soon as I said that, he exploded in me again. I could feel the warm cum entering my pussy.

We washed up and got out the shower. I went in the room and started to get dressed. Mike walked to the front door because the bell was ringing. I had no idea who it was; we never have company. I don't hang with nobody besides Jas, and Mike don't allow her over here when he's home because all they do is argue. Mike came back with a pizza and wings from Pizza Hut.

"Netflix and chill baby!?" Once again, I'm shocked. Other than fucking my brains out or beating my brains out, Mike never spent any quality time with me.

"Of course," I said with a smile on my face.

And just like that, it was like I had forgotten what he did to me this morning, even though I have the bruises to show for it.

Chapter 2

Mica

I woke up the next morning, and the house smelt delicious. Mike was making me breakfast. I was so happy because at the time I was so hungry. We pigged out on pizza, wings, and snacks the night before. But after so much sex and such a long night, I had slept for 11 hours and that almost never happens. Whatever he was cooking, I was going to smash when it's done.

"Baby, I forgot to grab orange juice," Mike said.

"Well you keep cooking, and I'll go grab some."

He looked at me with a big ass smile on his face. "That's my baby."

Not often do I see Mike smile, but he has the most perfect teeth I have ever seen, and his toned body and dark-skinned tone makes it so much better. I gave him a kiss, got dressed, applied a little bit of my makeup to cover over the beaten I got with the pistol, and headed to Walmart. I loved going shopping in the morning or late nights because no one is ever out that early or late. I pulled into Walmart to see the entire parking lot damn near filled. I slept too long and now it was 12pm. People were getting off work, running to Walmart during lunch breaks, going inside the bank inside Walmart. It was beyond busy.

There's a girl that works at Walmart name Cynthia. Every time I come here, she always mean mugging me like she knows me from somewhere or wants to square up. But like always, I ignore her ass. She has got to be one of Mike's hoes to be honest. I wouldn't be surprised. But like always when I walk in there, she goes staring me down. I was moving quickly because I didn't want her to notice my face was kind of bruised from when Mike pistol whipped me. I kept walking with my head down.

"Hey girl! How you been?" Cynthia said.

I have no idea why this bitch acting all friendly like she fucks with me; that's a typical nosey bitch move. I cannot stand females like her. I don't like you, and you don't like me. We don't have to be fake and speak to one another. I know how to be cordial. I'm not the rude type, so I spoke back.

"I been good," I said. I wasn't going to ask her how she been cause in all honesty, I really don't give a fuck.

"How Mike been?"

I immediately got pissed off. Why does it matter? Who's asking?

"Bitch, don't ask me about my man. That isn't none of your business. I was tryna be nice, but you are doing too muthafuckin much". I muffed her in the face and walked away, leaving her stunned.

Everyone that knows me knows I'm not rude nor a loud person, so I know she was as shocked as me to hear me talk like that. I know I shouldn't be calling Mike with no bullshit, but I just really needed to know.

Ring! Ring!

"Wassup baby," Mike said.

"Are you fucking this dusty ass bitch up here at Walmart?"

"What! What are u talking 'bout?"

"I'm talking about that trifling ass bitch Cynthia. Bitch just had the nerve to ask me how you been. I'm tired of being publicly humiliated because you don't know how to keep your dick in your goddamn pants, Mike. I'm sick of this shit."

"Baby, chill out! I'll handle that."

"YOU GONE HANDLE IT? Meaning you fucking her?"

"Hell naw, I'm not fucking her. Now chill out and bring that orange juice home."

Click.

What in the entire fuck does *'I'll handle it'* supposed to mean? Then he just hung up in my face, no "I love you", "drive safe", NOTHING. This is the careless shit that I'm done and over with.

I walked straight up to Cynthia. "You fucking Mike? This the last time I'm asking."

"What Mike say?"

This bitch keeps being funny like I won't knock her head between the cash register and shopping carts.

"Alright," is all I said. I walked off and dialed Wes' number.

"Where you at? Lemme slide thru."

"Aight creep."

On the way to Wes' crib, I kept trying to figure out what in the fuck was I doing. I should be bringing Mike this orange juice but fuck him. He gone continue to do me wrong until I put my foot down. Plus, this Ciara *I Bet* song is making me feel so much better.

'So, you bought me a car, he can buy that too. I can take care of myself & I can find someone to do it too. You act like you upgraded me, I upgraded you. You and me fashion week in Paris, I put you on the new.'

I was feeling every damn word she sang in my spirit. Now all I can think about is what Wes gone be wearing, & I'm already knowing his hazel eyes are going to make me melt. I can already hear him talking about, "Wassup creep." He been calling me creep for years, and I don't even know why.

I pulled up to his house and noticed a few cars outside. From the looks of it, looked and sounded like he was having a party. I called his cell.

"Wassup creep."

"You could have told me you were having a party. I didn't come for this shit. I'm going home."

"Man, hold up. I'm coming outside."

Click.

I wasn't just going to leave anyways. I knew he wasn't going to let me just leave. I been having Wes wrapped around my fingers for years. He gone always fuck with me. That's my forever and always, regardless of who else we end up with. We never slept together or anything, but we always remained to have this vibe about us that's unexplainable. I saw him walking towards the car, so I unlocked his door. I was trying so hard to hide the smile on my face and it's so crazy that after so many years this man can give me butterflies like a high school girl again. If I wasn't so chocolate, my cheeks would be bright red; seeing him is breathtaking.

He got in and slammed the door. "Girl, don't be bossing me around like that. Got me looking like a chump."

I started laughing. "Man, how you been? I haven't seen you in forever. You done forgot about me and shit."

"I could never forget about you. Matter fact, I'm gone have that nigga Mike touched; mark my words. I don't even know why you still messing with that goofy ass nigga."

I did not come here to talk about Mike, so now I'm so annoyed. I came because I missed him and just needed some personal time. Instead, he makes it about the person who pushed me to be here with him in the first place.

"Aight, Wes. Get back to your party. You're tripping."

"I'm not tripping. I love you girl, and you know that. But I'm sorry for bringing him up. Gimme a kiss tho."

I paused. I didn't know if I should kiss him, or not. So, he grabbed my face and stared me in my eyes for a good 25 seconds; instantly I fell in love. He then kissed me like no man has ever kissed me before. He kissed me like I was the only woman on this planet. He put his hands around my neck.

"Damn, I missed you," he said.

All I did was moan. He stopped and turned my car off. He got out the car, walked to my side opened my door, and walked me into the house. I wasn't worried about nobody there. I was just focused on Wes. He walked in front of me while holding my hand, leading the way. The way he walked turned me on. The way his body looked with clothes turn me on. I was so turned on, my hands started to sweat. He took me to his room and threw me on the bed.

He said "This pussy should have been mine, but you been playing games with me."

I just started laughing because that was the truth. I tried to grab his dick and suck it, but he pushed me back.

"Nah baby, I'm pleasing you. We can do that another time."

He dug his face between my legs and barely came up for breath. The things he did with his tongue was breath taking. My legs started to shake while I was poking my nails into his back. I started to cum.

"I'm cumming, Wes. Oh my fucking God!"

He wouldn't move his face. He started to eat it more, and I came all in his mouth. He finally came up and kissed me on my lips.

"This my last time saying it. You been mine. Fuck what you are talking about. That nigga Mike gone get his, and I don't wanna hear anything different."

We cuddled for the rest of the afternoon. I woke up at 6pm.

"OH SHIT! Wes, I forgot to take Mike this orange juice. He's going to kill me." I started to cry.

Wes grabbed my hands, "Aye relax. Let me take him the orange juice."

He grabbed my keys and walked out the door before I could even say anything

What the Fuck Did I Do?

****

Wes

Man, I can't believe this nigga been putting his hands on my baby girl. Her and I not together but that's some bitch ass shit, and I'll be damned if I let that shit slide. I bet she don't think I noticed her face being fucked up either. I've been with my fair share of woman, but Mica knows I love her and would body any nigga to protect her. She been with this nigga for seven years. Every time we crossed paths, she made it seem as if she had everything under control. The only person with control of anything was Mike over her. Why would he even want to bruise her precious body? Mica has got to be the most beautiful girl I have ever laid my eyes on. On my way to Mike, I started having flash backs to the day I first met Mica.

Jas had brought Mica over for a sleepover when they were in the 4th grade, and I was in the 5th grade. Even though we had went to the same elementary school, I still had never noticed her until she came to the house. She had on an overall short set with a long blue shirt underneath and some all-white forces. Her hair was styled into two pig tails with twists and burettes at the end. I had spent the entire day outside playing with friends and didn't even notice that Jas had brought her over. Mom called me inside for dinner, and when I got to the table, I laid eyes on Mica.

"Boy, pick your jaws up!" My mother yelled.

She was sitting right next to my seat. I was sweating and getting nervous. We all ate dinner and towards the end, Mica accidently rubbed her foot against my leg, and I immediately got a hard dick. I had never experienced this before, so it scared me. My mom asked me to get up and get the ice trays out the freezer, and I wouldn't move.

"Wes, get your narrow ass up and do what I said."

When I stood up from the table, my mom's mouth dropped, and her eyes got big which made Jas and Mica look as well.

"Cover yawl eyes. Boy, go to your goddamn room!"

I was embarrassed. Ever since, I have been crazy about her.

"Wait till I get a hold of that fool ass nigga," I mumbled under my breath while driving.

I was speeding down Chicago ave trying to make it to her crib, they crib, or the hell hole he been keeping her stranded and trapped in.

Ring. Ring. Ring.

It was Mica calling me. "Wassup my beautiful creep"

"How can you sound so normal and sweet knowing you about to go do some crazy shit, Wes?"

"I sound normal because you with me is normal. I called you beautiful because that's what you are. I'ma call you back when I'm on my way back home. Call my sister and tell her I said come by with my credit card and take you shopping. Get whatever you want, baby."

"Awe… look at you, balling and shit," she said.

"Anything for my Queen. I'll get back to you in a little, won't take me long. I love you."

Click.

I hung up quick. Since me and Mica have known one another, I have never told her I loved her and to be honest, it just kind of slipped out this time too. Jas and Mica been friends for years, so I knew that calling Jas to go shopping would calm her down a little. I pulled into Mica's driveway, parked the car, and walked to the door.

Knock Knock

"What the hell take you so lo..." is all Mike could get out his mouth before I tried to punch his teeth down his throat. He stumbled into the room, and I closed the door behind me. He just looked filthy. Hair all over his head, hair all over his face. He was a lot more in shape 7 years ago. Looks like he been drinking beer since high school. The man really had let himself go.

"I ain't take too long, nigga. I'm right on time. Get yo ass up and look at me like a man."

"Bro, what the fuck? What's that for?"

"That's for the black eye that Mica walking around with. What's about to happen next is for my pleasure. Now sit yo ass down on that couch."

He looked so soft. It's always the abusive niggas who scared of other actual niggas. I plan on making him pay for every hit he ever laid on Mica. I plan on making him a better man with this ass whooping because when I'm done with him, he's not going to want to put his hand on another woman in this world. I never liked him. Not only because of Mica, but for my own personal reasons.

"Why is it that you can bully her around but you ain't tried shit with me since I hit you in your shit?"

"Man, that's between me and Mica. I love her, and she knows that."

This nigga must think I'm stupid or something, talking about he loves her. This shit is not love. You don't black the eye of a woman you supposed to love. You don't hurt the woman you suppose to love. When the love is real, it just is. You don't have to justify it with other bullshit. Love should not feel forced, and love should not leave you scarred. The way Mica woke up with terror in her voice, scared because she forgot to bring this bitch ass nigga some damn orange juice, I knew it was time to get rid of his ass for good.

"Nigga, you don't love her."

Bloop

I hit him in his shit. "Next time you lie to my face, it's gone be worse. So, does hitting her make you feel more of a man? You feel powerful? Strong? Unstoppable?

Does it make the sex better? Like, please tell me what you had running through yo head when you did this shit, G."

I'm considering killing this nigga right now, but I'ma give him the benefit of the doubt and give him a chance to explain himself to me. Mica is my heart; I love that girl to death. Killing him won't make her closer to me. I wouldn't even do that for that reason. I know that she doesn't want him dead, so imma spare him but imma make sure he moves around in a timely fashion.

"Man, I'm sorry. I won't do it again," Mike said.

I know this nigga probably told Mica this a million times. That's usually what weak niggas do. He was quick to lay hands on her and now I'm right here in his face pulling his card, and he turns into a bitch.

"Aight, hear me out. I will give you 24 hours to get your shit out her crib, and stay the fuck away from her. If I find out you so much as walked around the corners of this crib, imma snap your muthafuckin neck and not think twice about it."

After I said that, I spat in his face. I never spit on people, but he is a piece of shit, and I don't have an ounce of respect for anyone like him. I can't wait for him to try Mica again, so I can fuck his shit up. I grabbed an outfit out the closet for Mica and left Mike sitting there with blood dripping from his face.

"You think she would wear this color today?"

He just looked at me stuck, and I walked out.

On the drive back to my crib, my face was lit up and my smile was huge. I couldn't wait to get home and hold my baby. I was finally going to have her to myself. It was my turn to treat her how she should have been treated. It was finally a real nigga turn. I stopped at Walmart and grabbed a dozen of roses just to surprise her. I didn't know if she was gone shopping with Jas yet or still at my crib, so I called her.

Ring Ring

"Hello?"

"Creep, don't be answering your phone like you don't know who I am. Where you at?

"I'm still at your crib. Please tell me you ain't do nothing crazy, Wes."

"Do I look like the type of nigga that do crazy shit?"

"Hell yeah!" We both started laughing hella hard and hella loud.

"Aight, I see you got jokes. Call Jas and tell her don't come. I'm on my way back to you.

"Aight, bye."

I would have loved to tell Mica I loved her before she hung up the phone. I have loved her since I was a child. I'm pretty sure she knows that already though. I can't wait to see what the future has in store for us.

"Damn! Can't wait to see my baby," I said under my breath.

Chapter 3

Mike

I can't believe she sent that nigga to my house. I know I'm wrong for hitting her, but Mica just makes me so mad. She questions everything I do and say. Shit. It's not an excuse to hit her, but she been used to this shit. We been doing this for years! As I was packing up my clothes to get ready to leave, I start crying because I know she about to be with that nigga and playing house and shit. Mica knows that she belongs to me. I was her first and nobody can take my place. imma just give her a lil time to think and cool off, but I'm most definitely coming back to get my girl. After seven years, it should not be that easily for her to get over me. I helped her when she had nothing. I molded her into the woman she has become. I know her body inside and out. I know how she likes to be fucked. I know what to buy her to make her feel better. I know exactly what she's going to order at every restaurant that we go to. I know that woman like no other.

I call up my home boy Sean. "Aye dawg, where you at?"

"In the hood, what's good?" He said. Sean was always ready for war, and when he hears about this Wes nigga, he gone be ready to shoot.

"We got some business to handle. imma slide by you in a second."

"Aight, one love," Sean said before hanging up.

This nigga done came in my crib, took my bitch and told me I got to get out of my shit? I don't think he knows what kind of monster he just woke up. I pulled up on Sean and he was sitting on the porch. This nigga is really the definition of a hood nigga. I'm from out south, and Sean from out west, but we been partners for years because we grew up together. I couldn't stand coming to his crib. It be entirely too hot over there. He lives off Chicago Ave and West Huron.

"Washannin my nigga!" Sean yelled before I got out of my car.

"A whole lot of fuck shit. I need you to let me crash over here for a few days while I stack this money and get back on my feet."

"Damn, what happen? Shorty ass put yo dumbass out, huh?"

"Nah, the nigga she fucking off with did."

Sean started laughing. "Man, what did you just say? A nigga put you out yo own crib?"

"Man, you know that nigga Wes who got the little sister named Jas?"

"Yeah, what about 'em?"

"He been feeling Mica way before her and I got together. To make a long story short, she ended up being mine and the nigga been sick ever since. You know how me and Mica get down. We fight, argue and all that shit, but the last fight, she damn near tried to kill me. Pulled the trigger and all but wasn't no bullets in that bitch. The fact that she was really about to just start bussing on me pissed me off so bad, I took the gun from her, and pistol whipped her."

"Dawg, you lying. It ain't never get that deep."

"Blood, I promise you, if I could take the shit back I would. You know I love that girl, Blood."

"Yeah, all that hallmark ass shit sound good, but we gone have to do something about this nigga Celest."

We both knew he said the nigga name all wrong and started laughing. We smoked a couple blunts and talked shit to all the bitches walking up and down the block for the rest of the night.

****

Mica

I know Wes left to go do some crazy shit, and quite frankly, I don't even care! It's been a long seven years of getting my ass beat, being lied to and cheated on.

Enough is enough, and Wes made that clear when he gave me no option but to wait until he got back from handling Mike. After he called me and told me he was on his way back, I started to feel butterflies all through my stomach and just wanted him to hurry up. I felt like a 14-year-old girl again except my Prince Charming wasn't Mike, it was Wes. I could not wait to see him again. In the back of my mind, I was worried for Mike. I knew exactly what Wes was capable of before letting him go drop the orange juice off.

"Aye Baby!" I heard Wes say from outside the window.

I peeked my head out. "Boy, why you screaming and acting like we Romeo and Juliet?"

He laughed, "Come downstairs!" I haven't left his room since he left, and I knew there were people in the living room, so I tried to move as quickly as possible.

Once I got outside, Wes' perfect smile started glowing like I was the only girl in the world that mattered to him; like he was ready to ask me to marry him; like he just didn't get done nearly killing Mike, if he already hadn't.

I walked up to him and gave him a big ass kiss. "Damn, daddy. Took you long enough," I tried to say in a sexy voice which made him laugh. This all seemed so right yet so corny to me. Wes and I have never been on an intimate level like this, and in a way… I never thought we would. But damn ain't I happy that we are.

"Damn, mama! Why you ain't call and check on me? I could have been getting my ass beat."

I just punched him in his chest. He knows damn well ain't nobody in Chicago fucking with him. There were a lot of nut ass niggas in this city, but Wes put the icing on the cake and tops it all off. Wes was the kind of nigga that walks into a room, and everyone notices him. His presence speaks volume. He made niggas that were loud seem quiet.

"No, but on a serious tip, how you feel about moving out that place yawl was living in?"

"And move where?" I said, turning around and looking at the house he lived in. I can't handle people walking in and out and being in my space, so that would never work for me.

Wes looked at me and smiled. "Get in the car. Let's go for a ride," still not answering my question. I gave him the look like *no!* Seriously, I'm not moving in that house with all those damn people. I don't even know the people inside that house. It reminds me of a trap house minus the filth and drugs.

We drove for an entire hour to go on the outskirts of Chicago into the suburbs. We pulled up to the most beautiful house I have ever seen. My mouth immediately dropped when I saw the for-sale sign in the yard. Wes came over to my side of the car, opened my door and handed me a set of keys. "Go check it out."

This house literally looked like my dream home and it was so big. "Who house is this?"

"It could be ours if you wanted it to be," Wes said.

"Are you serious? Me and you just got back talking today, and you haven't even asked me to be your girlfriend yet," I said with a smile on my face.

"Baby, you been my girl since I was in the 5th grade. So, are you going to start over with me and let me treat you like the queen you are, or are you going to act like you don't love this big ass house?"

"Wes, why do you have this house? When did you get this?" I said, looking concerned.

"Months ago, because I was just gonna move here by myself and try to get custody of Karisma."

Karisma is Wes' only daughter and only child. She was put into foster care when her mother was arrested on some petty theft charges. He couldn't get her because he was still a felon and on house arrest for a while. I've been telling Wes to try to get her for years. I know firsthand how that foster care life can go, and no child should ever have to be put through any of it. It's worse because she's younger than I was when I ended up a victim of the system. I was 12, and Karisma is 5. They can easily manipulate her young mind. I can't wait for Wes to get custody of her.

"Well, I love this house, and I love the idea you have," I said.

I walked to him and gave him a kiss. Within one day, I went from being pistol whipped to owning a home and being a stepmother. What have I gotten myself into?

I was never shown how a man should treat a woman. Not from my father, nor a family member, let alone the nigga I spent seven years with. So be a little understanding when I say my choices in men are not all that great. Mike was a terrible person and did terrible things to me that I have also gotten use to because he's been doing them for a long time and never tried to cover them up. Mike was toxic for me. We had great sex, and a great time when things were going well. However, when things got bad, things were all the way fucked up. Now Wes, on the other hand, has secrets, and he literally will take them to the grave before admitting them.

Only a month deep into this new relationship, and I'm already having doubts. Wes has money and I was always taught that all money is not good money! Within this month, everything has been moving fast. He doesn't have custody of Karisma yet, but we have been getting her every weekend. She loves the house and she loves me. I treat her as if she was my daughter because that's what you do when you're in a relationship with someone with children that are not yours. Karisma and I painted her bedroom walls pink and decorated her entire room the way she wanted. Her vision is everything because her room turned out amazing. She doesn't have a theme like most kids would want; it's just colorful and very girly. She loved my makeup vanity and playing in makeup. Therefore, me and Wes built her a kid makeup vanity, and now that's all she wants to do.

But let's fast forward to me explaining how fishy Wes has been acting. He's coming home all different kind of hours of the night, and I just feel it in my gut something is wrong. Wes doesn't want to stress me about anything because I'm a pregnant. Little does he know, I don't even think this child is his. Me and him got together right after Mike exploding inside my pussy. Ever since me and Wes got together, he hasn't pulled out once when we make love. I mean, he can't be mad if I'm pregnant by Mike because we did hop into this RIGHT after me and Mike ended. I don't know when I'm going to tell him, or if I'm ever going to tell him. Maybe he already knows and that's why he's been acting so distant towards me. I can't believe that I'm about to be a mother. Two months ago, I would have found the nearest abortion clinic and got rid of this baby in a heartbeat. Wes is different though. I know he will be a great father because I already see it first hand with Karisma.

Anyways, I got dressed and did my makeup and hair cute tonight. Wes told me we were having a date night. I looked forward to nights like this because it was just me and him. He is already an hour late coming back home to pick me up, so I'm getting a bit agitated that he wouldn't call and let me know instead of letting me sit here twiddling my thumbs. My pregnancy hormones have had so irate lately that sometimes *I* don't even want to be in the same room as *me*.

BEEP BEEP

Wes was outside blowing the horn. He went from opening doors for me to blowing his horn at me like I was one of those crack head ass addicts he serves. I not in the business of pissing Wes off, because we know how far that got with Mike. I doubt that Wes would ever put his hands on me, but I don't put it pass anyone. I got in the car and gave Wes a kiss. I guess you could call me submissive. I just didn't want to chance it. I've had my fair share of ass whooping's, so I hold my tongue and don't say or do anything that would piss Wes off.

"Baby girl, we can't catch that movie and dinner tonight because some shit been going down lately, so I'm headed to the trap. You can come with me if you'd like?"

With him creeping in and out the house in the middle of the night and claiming that he's working, I wanted to see what he really be up to and who he around. The look on his face when I said I was coming told me something was up. It was like he expected me to say, 'No, its fine, handle your business.' Nope! I want to go and see shit for myself. That's the incentive of being with an abusive piece of shit. I peep bullshit a lot quicker than I would have in the past and the signs of fuckery are clearer to me these days.

Sure enough, we pull up to the trap, and I already spot some skanky hoes sitting on the porch; one by the name of Cynthia. I'm starting to think this bitch is obsessed with me and what's mine. First, she all up on Mike. Now she in Wes' face and around where he be around. She's not even a southsider. I just wanna slam her on her back, but I'm pregnant, so I let that thought exit my mind quickly.

I walked up the porch holding Wes' hand.

"Hey Wes," Cynthia said, not even acknowledging me, or that I was there.

And Wes had the audacity to respond to that bitch, not saying *hey*, but this nigga said "Wassup shorty". I ain't never heard this nigga calling a bitch shorty since I've known him, but I kept calm and let that shit slide. I tried to walk with him into the house before Wes stopped me.

"Nah baby. Wait out here. Too many niggas in there." I understand that he didn't want me around a bunch of niggas, but I damn sure didn't want to be sitting on the porch with this bald head ass bitch Cynthia.

"Girl, you move on quick," Cynthia said.

I ignored her cause Lord knows being pregnant my temper can get bad and I'm trying not to act out in front of all Wes's people.

"I'm starting to wonder what's wrong with your pussy that every man that you move on to tends to still want to fuck the shit out of me."

This bitch is getting bold and just pretty much admitting to fucking my man. I started laughing. "Well did you enjoy the dick?" Is all I said.

I got up and walked inside the house, grabbed Wes and told him I needed to go home. He asked why, and I told him I was feeling fatigued. He gave me the car keys and said call him when I made it home safe. As I got in the car, I seen Cynthia walking as if she was leaving. I reached back under Wes' car seat, grabbed his gun and followed her. I stopped the car and beeped.

"Girl, you do not have to walk home. Catch a ride with me," I said in the fakest voice humanly possible.

I knew she would ride with me because she wouldn't expect me to do anything crazy. I was known for being the sweetest girl everyone knew and loved.

"Idk where you headed but Wes' daughter is being dropped off and I have to run by the house and scoop her. You fine to ride with?"

"Yeah girl. I ain't got nothing to do," she replied

I'm thinking in my head, *you should be running.* We pulled up to the house and Cynthia started acting like every ghetto ass hood rat. "Girl, this house big as shit. You done came up." Blah blah blah! She was acting real fucking pressed like she ain't never been outside of the hood.

"You wanna walk in and check it out?" I said.

"Hell, yeah girl!"

I showed her the entire house. Then I told her how the basement was my woman cave, so we started walking down there. Once we got down there, she noticed it wasn't shit in the basement. I pulled Wes' gun out.

"Bitch, get on your knees." She did exactly as I said. "Old me with Mike would have let your comments with me slide. New me with Wes will blow your fucking brains out."

BOOM! Didn't even give her a chance to explain herself; these crazy relationships and crazy niggas are making me into a monster. A monster that I'm growing to love. I called Mike.

"I need you to come help me move this body."

"On my way," he said.

No questions asked. No hesitation. Mike was on his way period!

Chapter 4

Mica

I know you're thinking why the fuck am I back around this nigga? Haven't I learned my lesson? The truth of the matter is, I am not with him or sleeping with him; I haven't touched, kissed, or did anything with Mike since the day Wes snatched me up. But Mike will do anything for me, besides not putting his hands on me. You would think my first time killing someone that I would be shook up and flustered. No, I was calm as shit, and I feel a lot better now that she's dead. The bitch had it coming. She kept coming for me when she wasn't sent for, now look at her; can't talk shit no more. Believe it or not, Mike is the reason I'm all heartless and shit. I'd rather get them before they get me. I will never wait for someone to beat my ass ever again. I was looking out the window when Mike pulled up. He had to be speeding because he made it to my house in 15 mins on a 45 min drive. He came to the door and I opened it.

"Man, don't tell me this nigga got you out here putting muthafuckas in body bags. This ain't you, Mica. Fuck is going on?"

Why is this nigga questioning me? Like, if you were so concerned, how come your bitch ass don't question Wes. Him asking questions really annoyed the shit out of me! Him and I both know that talking shit about Wes won't get him nowhere but in a grave, but knowing Mike, he is moving silently. As much history me and him have, I wouldn't mind whacking him to make sure no harm comes to my baby. Wes and I ain't been together that long but ultimately, I feel like my heart was meant to be with him. Of course I got some questions about what connections him and this Cynthia bitch got going on, and I'm going to get answers regardless.

Mike and I put Cynthia's body in his trunk and went to the basement to clean the blood up. Thank God my floors aren't carpet. After we were done, I asked Mike where he planned to take the body, and he said the less I know, the safer I am. He ain't got to tell me twice; I'd rather be as clueless as possibly. If this shit got out that Cynthia was killed, and Mike was the suspect in the murder, would I cover his ass or take the bid? Hell, the fuck no! My name Bennett and I ain't in it! I walked Mike to his car and told him I appreciate the help. I done left him for a whole new nigga, and I still got him wrapped around my fingers.

"Mica man, promise you gone stay safe. What you think you know about this nigga ain't all the truth. He isn't who you think he is, Mica. He's been lying to you and hiding mad shit from you."

"What's that supposed to mean? And nigga, I'm not your baby!" I said concerned.

"Just trust me. There's shit that I can't talk about, but I'm telling you right now you need to figure out a way out and get rid of this nigga."

I didn't know what he meant by that, and quite frankly I didn't care. Me and Wes are like Bonnie and Clyde. That's my forever boy, and can't nobody say shit that would make me change my mind about our love. I would never turn on him, he would never turn on me and that fact that Mike expects that, blows me.

"That bitch in the trunk of your car was murdered because you fucked her while with me and gave this bitch a reason to think I was a joke. So, trust you? You want me to trust you? Only thing I trust is that you'll make sure this body doesn't get traced back to me. Don't you ever question shit about my man."

I left him in the drive way and walked in the house. I heard a loud ass ringtone. I knew it wasn't my phone, so I automatically thought Mike left his phone. It was sitting on the couch the name calling said "Bae"

I answered and stayed quiet. All I heard was, "Baby, where you go? Mica went home."

The caller was Wes....

Did his number say "Bae" in that bitch's phone? I kept repeating that answer in my head a million times. I realized I needed to get rid of the phone before he came home, seen it and knew something was up. Then again, should I keep it, so he doesn't realize that she's missing? But what the fuck do he mean *baby, where you at*? Just when you think someone's perfect, they prove you all the way wrong! I honestly can't believe this shit. Cynthia so fucking dusty; what did him or Mike see in this bitch? I cleaned up the house good, showered, made him some dinner and waited for him to come home. I wasn't sure if I was going to confront him tonight or make him eventually tell me.

No, fuck that! We are confronting this shit tonight. I grabbed that dusty ass android and put it right under his pillow case in the bedroom. I was walking back to the living room when I heard the door open, I walked over to him and gave him a kiss like I always do. And just like every cheating ass nigga, he kissed me back like he wasn't trying to fuck on some ratchet pussy. I kept cool because I knew exactly how I was going to get back at him. We ate dinner, he told me was going to wash the dishes. While I'm lying in the bed, I can hear this nigga blowing her phone up while I'm laying right next to it. He had common sense not to come in this room texting or calling another bitch, so I knew he wouldn't notice right away that the phone was under his pillow. I grabbed the phone out and made sure the notification volume was all the way up to the point that it could wake me up out of my sleep.

Wes came in the room and started undressing. He was completely naked when he walked over to me, said, "I'll be back", and walked into our bathroom in our bedroom.

I tried my hardest to stay up and not fall asleep, but he was taking too long. At 2am in the morning, I woke up with his head between my thighs; I'm starting to believe he has a fetish for eating pussy. He was going to work on my clit. I instantly wanted to explode in his mouth. My legs were shaking so bad to the point that he had to hold them above my head to keep them up. I'm nothing but 140 lbs. and 5 feet, so Wes was able to bend and turn me any way that he wanted to. I grabbed his head, pushed it harder into my pussy and then came all in his mouth. He got up and I tried to get out the bed to clean up my juices. He grabbed me and threw me on the bed.

"Where you think you going?" He said. I moaned louder as he stuck his dick in my pussy, then took it out, then stuck it again, teasing the hell out of me. I was scared at this moment that someone was going to call Cynthia's phone, but that bitch is a nobody. I highly doubted it, so I continued to get my second nut. Wes was fucking me so hard, he kept slapping my ass to the point where it stung. We have never been this aggressive before, but it's kind of turning me on more. He pulled out and told me to get on the floor on my knees. He came all in my mouth. I've never swallowed before, but he told me to swallow, so that's exactly what I did. He grabbed my hand and helped me get off the ground and kissed me.

"That's my baby," he said.

I'm thinking in my head, *yeah yeah yeah whatever*. We laid back in the bed and he cuddled me until I fell asleep. I turned over towards him at 6am in the morning, and he was texting on his phone. He couldn't tell that I was looking because I was peeking. When he finally sent a text to Cynthia's phone, he realized her phone was under his head. He got up and nugged me to wake up.

"WHY THE FUCK IS CYNTHIA PHONE UNDER MY PILLOW, MICA?"

I calmly said, "Why the fuck are you texting her at 6 in the morning? What's so important to talk about, Wes!?"

"Mica, stop playing with me. What did you do to her?"

"Oh, you miss your little baby, huh? She's dead!" I said.

And in that moment, I realized Wes loved this bitch because he started crying. He got me fucked up! I couldn't believe this nigga was in front of me balling his eyes out over this bitch. There must be more to the story then what I'm being told. This the type of shit Mike was talking about when he said there's things about Wes that I don't know. Can't wait till I talk to Mike. I'm going to cuss his ass out if he knew anything about this.

"So, you in love with that bitch? That's why you're crying?" I asked Wes.

"No baby, I'm not in love with her. There's just things you don't know and won't understand."

That was complete bullshit. How the fuck does he know what I would understand and not understand? It's like pushing me away without even giving me a chance. I have never judged him or anything, so that coming out his mouth is beyond shocking.

"When have I ever judged you? But if you love me like you say you do, I advise you to start telling me what the hell is going on, Wes!" I yelled.

"You love Karisma, right?"

I didn't understand why the fuck he was bringing up his daughter. "Yes, of course."

"Then why you kill her mother, Mica?"

WHAT? Her mother? Ok, when he said it was some shit that I won't understand, he was right. Cause me trying to put two and two together is damn near not making sense.

"What do you mean Cynthia is her mother?"

"Cynthia is the girl I got pregnant. She didn't wanna keep the baby because she felt like she was too young, so she carried her and gave her up to me for full custody. I was dating Nyla at the time, so she took her in as her own and been saying she was her baby ever since.

We even got some connects in the system to get her birth certificate switched."

These mother fuckers are nuts. Who does that? I'm supposed to feel sorry for a bitch who neglected the child that she created? I put her out her misery. She was a miserable ass bitch.

"Well Wes, we not about to sit here and cry. She's dead. She crossed me one too many times"

"Mica, what the fuck is wrong with you? When did you become so damn heartless? How did you even get rid of the damn body?"

I knew he was going to ask that because my tiny ass wouldn't be able to carry shit by myself. I just laughed. "I had Mike come over and help me. He told me the less I know the safer I will be."

"And he thought it as safe to bring his bitch ass in my house?"

I just ignored his question. "Only reason I ain't killed that nigga yet is because Karisma might actually be his daughter," Wes said.

My mouth dropped. *What the fuck do he mean?* "WHAT?" I yelled.

"Yeah. Cynthia was fucking on both of us at the time of her getting pregnant, and I was pressing her about who was the father. That's when she decided to give my baby up for adoption. I told her there's still a fifty percent chance she was my baby, so I'll take her. I never asked or talked about it again because regardless, Karisma is my daughter."

Mike deserves to know if he has a 4-year-old daughter. I'm going to tell him.

"And you better not say shit about it, Mica."

I thought to myself, *You shouldn't have told me anything about it.*

Chapter 5

Wes

I don't know if I'm mad or more so disappointed in Mica. She been going nuts lately and I ain't about to let her blame it on pregnancy hormones. Then again, I feel a lot better knowing she shot Cynthia before fighting her because she could have lost my baby. It took everything in me not to smack her upside her head. Can you blame me? She just murdered my child's mother. But then again, she didn't know anything about Cynthia being Karisma's mom. I'm not even an abusive ass nigga, but she most definitely took me there. She thinking she don't know me at all anymore and the way she been acting got me feeling like I never once knew her. This is not what I fell in love with. Not to mention she fucked me last night like nothing even happened. Mica may be a little bipolar; something's not adding up. I was never in love with Cynthia, but how can you not have love for the woman who birthed your child? And when I did my bid, Cynthia was there for me the entire two years. I find myself steady calling her phone, knowing she won't pick up. I was driving my 2005 Cadillac around the city when I got a call from a number I don't know.

"Who this?"

"That's how you greet the woman of yo dreams?" It was Nyla; she must be out of jail now.

"Girl, when they let you out?" I said, laughing.

"Don't worry about that. Slide on me really quick. I'm in the PJ's."

The Pj's was a short way of saying projects. I knew Nyla being out wouldn't be good because she's in love with me, and she has no clue that I'm with Mica. I pulled up and she was already outside being praised by the entire projects for being back home. She hopped in my car and tried to give me a kiss, but I stopped her.

"There's some things we have to talk about," I said.

"Yeah, like how come you ain't came to visit me the last month I was in."

"Nyla, me and Mica together. We been rocking for a good month. I just need you to know that so neither one of yawl think I'm hiding anything, and I'm going to let her know you out."

"Wasn't she with Mike? How you gone hop into a relationship without ending the one you were in because a bitch was in jail?" Nyla said, very upset.

I don't even know why she is tripping. Her and I were not together; we were co-parenting. This what happens when you nice to women who have feelings for you. They automatically think yawl go together.

"Anyways, la 'daddy I already knew about all that. Tell Mica I hope she have a safe pregnancy."

How the fuck did when she find out? And who the fuck told her? Things are about to get ugly quicker than I can blink.

****

Mica

After Wes left out because he was mad I bodied his baby momma, which I didn't know was his baby momma, I started to feel bad. I understand now why it affected him, but she was a dead-beat mother doing dicks and not knowing the father. Half the south side of Chicago could be Karisma's daddy! I started laughing thinking about it cause my life went from not interesting to all this drama; I kind of like it. Wes texted my phone and told me he was on his way back home, and it sounded kind of urgent. So, I waited for him to get back then my phone rang.

"Wassup girl?" I said. It was Jas calling me.

"Girl, how you been? You done shacked up with Wes and forgot all about me."

We both started laughing cause it's kind of true. Between being pregnant, fucking all the time and arguing, I been beyond busy. "Girl, I missed you. We should hang out, maybe hit downtown up, but you know my pregnant ass can't drink."

"Aight, bet. I'll pick you up around 9 tonight." We said goodbye to each other then hung up.

Wes walked in the house after I put my phone on the charger. Even tho I knew he was mad at me, he had the look in his eyes like he wanted to eat my pants off me.

"Baby, we need to talk. I just wanna know have you ever killed anyone else, because you doing this is shocking to me."

"No, Wes. I have never killed anyone," I said, rolling my eyes. "Have you ever killed anyone?"

"You know I've had a few muthafuckas killed, but I've only killed one person."

"Who?" I said.

"Some dude I used to get work from. One day I got robbed and he charged at me, so I killed him. It was only to save my life because he was going to take mine."

I understood where he was coming from because this street life can get hectic, and niggas get killed every day doing the shit that he does. "So, anything else we need to talk about?" I said before walking up to him and unzipping his pants.

"Nah, that was it, baby."

I took his dick out his pants, wrapped my lips around it and started sucking it. I made sure it was soaked because Wes loves sloppy ass head.

He grabbed my head and yelled out, "Damn, baby!"

Whenever he talked to me and let it be known he liked it, it made me go harder. I started deep throating his dick. He grabbed my head and held it still.

"I'm about to bust, baby." I stayed there with his dick all the way down my throat. He came so hard in my mouth, his ass cheeks started to clench the couch cushions.

When we were done, Wes went in the bedroom and took a nap because he knew on a Friday night if his phone rang, he will never get any sleep. I got on my phone and started to do some research.

'Man killed on the 100th block of Halsted is Leroy Smith.'

The man Wes killed was my father.

I can't believe what I just discovered. My father died when I was 18, so that means Wes was 20. I didn't find out Leroy was my father till after he died, and I never spoke about it, but I didn't know that Wes was the one that killed him. I kept my cool because I was never that close to my dad to get too mad like that. I woke Wes up and told him I was about to shower and get dressed to hit the club with Jas. He was cool with it and gave me a kiss. A normal kiss, like he didn't kill my father.

I was not showing that bad yet, so I put on a black dress with some pumps and a choker, it's been awhile since I been out with my girl. It's time to kick back and have some fun. I would be getting sloppy drunk if I wasn't pregnant.

BEEP BEEP

I heard Jas beeping outside, so I gave Wes a kiss and told him I loved him. We headed downtown to a bar named Spades. I was standing with Jas by the bar because she was having a drink when Nyla walked up behind her. Boy was I surprised. I thought she had another 7-8 months left. I wonder why they let her out early. I said hey, and she spoke back. I was not going to be rude to her because me and Nyla never had an issue. We were never friends, and never kicked it or anything. Therefore, me and Wes being together shouldn't bother her much at all.

Nyla is beautiful. She's brown skinned just like me, so I guess you could say Wes has a type. She's a little bit taller than me, maybe 5'2 and we're about the same size. She has some long bundles in her hair and wore a bright red dress that fit her body like a glove. She is stunning, I don't even understand why Wes would leave her for me. Although we have a lot physically in common, we're nothing alike. I'm laid back, calm and collected most of the time. Nyla, on the other hand, is a hot head. She's ready to pop off at any given moment with whoever. I've heard about a few fights she has gotten into, but it doesn't scare me none. I know what I'm capable of. That's what makes me and her so different. She talks way too much about a whole lot of nothing. I sit back and observe and pop off when needed to and the right times. That's why her and Wes probably attached to one another. They both love the limelight and never know how to sit in the background. They love having their names in everyone's mouth.

"I just seen Wes earlier. Congrats on the baby by the way."

Jas interrupted her and asked if she wanted a drink, but she declined. We proceeded to catch up.

"So, how's my daughter been since you been playing house with her?" Nyla said.

I'm starting to wonder why she was coming at me hostile. I ain't did nothing wrong. I've been taking great care of her "daughter" while she was behind bars stealing shit like Wes a broke nigga and wouldn't buy her whatever she wanted.

"Karisma has been good. I actually taught her her ABC's," I shot back. If this bitch wanted to play this salty role, I could go right along with her. Jas excused herself to go to the bathroom.

"I'm home and I want my life back, including my man. I'll give you time to ponder on that," Nyla said to me and walked away.

Was she threatening me? I think she still thinks I'm this innocent ass girl, but I'm not. I'll put her body right next to Cynthia's if she tries to come between me and Wes. She could have Mike, but Wes not an option.

I got up and walked away from the bar towards the bathroom to find Jas.

"Girl, they not going to last long and that baby ain't even my brother's," I heard Jas saying to Nyla.

My best friend turned on me. My best friend is plotting on me. For what reason? I don't know. I walked out the club, got in a taxi and cried the whole ride home. I couldn't believe what I just heard. I would never do that to her. We been friends since the 3rd grade, and this is how she does me. I guess it's true what they say. Watch who you call your friends.

I finally made it home and Wes was walking out. He seen me crying, so he stopped me and asked what was wrong with me. I told him all about how I was at the club and Nyla showed up then how Jas was plotting on me, telling that bitch all our goddamn business.

"So, Jas the one telling our business to Nyla because I was trying to figure how she knew the shit she knew in the first place," Wes said. I could tell he was heated. Me nor him expected Jas to betray us like this. I'm her best friend and he's her brother. What strings does this bitch got her hanging from?

"Baby, I'm going to handle it. Don't even worry about it" he said before giving me a kiss on my forehead and hopping in his car.

I knew he would handle it. I still didn't want him to do anything crazy. However, I knew if I handled it, I would most definitely do something beyond crazy. I'm pregnant, so it's best if I don't risk it.

Once I got in the house, I showered and called Mike.

"Where you at?" I asked.

"At my momma crib," he said dryly.

"Well, I'm about to pull up. I need to talk to you."

When I got over there, Mike seemed like he didn't want to talk to me nor was he even happy to see me.

"I'm pregnant," I said.

"I know."

"I don't know if the baby is yours or his, but I just thought you should know."

"That's cool, Mica. Be with him. Hopefully it's his child. Ever since u got with that nigga, bad things been coming my way. And why the fuck would you tell him I helped you move Cynthia's body?" He yelled.

"What happened, Mike?"

"For starters, niggas been shooting at me like crazy, and me and you both know it's because of that nigga. My nigga Sean from out west wanna get at him, but out of respect for you, I called it off."

I didn't argue with him on that because Wes did say, '*And he thought it was safe to bring his ass to my house?*' All I told Mike was that even tho I love Wes, he still needs to protect himself. Mike proceeded to tell me how much he loves me and whenever I "wake up" and snap back into reality that he will be here for me. It's kind of ironic that he says that seeing how when I was "waking", he was always beating my ass like I was a punching bag.

"Well I just wanted to tell you all that. I'm going to head home. This baby been taking all of my energy and making me so tired," I said, whining.

Mike grabbed my hand, pulled me closer to him and kissed me. Kissed me like he has never kissed me before. Part of me wanted him to stop, but the way my hormones been set up, I could not resist him. He trailed from my lips to my neck. It felt amazing. Suddenly, he stopped.

"Mica, take care of yo self and take care of that baby," he said before getting out the car. He literally got me hot and bothered to just leave me high and dry. I was seconds away from asking him to take me in that house and fuck me in every way possible. If he would have wanted more, I would have given him it all.

Call me crazy, but Mike has been changing a lot, and I can see it. It's kind of like me being with Wes humbled him. I started driving home and made it 5 minutes from Mike's house when I had to pull over because ambulances were speeding down the street. I immediately called his phone and got no answer. I sped the 5 minutes all the way back to his house and seen him lying on the ground wounded. Blood was everywhere. He was not moving or anything.

He didn't even make it all the way in the house after getting out of my car. I knew I should have watched him walk in the house.

No one could have done this but one person. This has Wes written all over it.

Chapter 6

Mica

I was speeding home to see if Wes was home or not. I kept calling his phone, but he was not answering. Tears boiled up, and I broke down while driving. Mike did terrible things to me, but this was shocking. Seeing him laid out like that in front of my eyes killed my soul. I loved Mike, regardless of everything he had done to. After Seven years with that man, I would never wish any harm upon him. I tried to call Wes one more time, but I was getting an incoming call from Jas.

"BITCH YOU HAVE SOME NERVE!" I yelled into the phone. I took all my built-up anger out on her. She deserved it for betraying me like she did with Nyla.

"Imma need for you to watch your mouth. What's wrong with you?"

"Where do I start off? That I left the club an hour and a half ago and u just now calling, or that I overheard you and that bitch Nyla plotting on me. We been home girls since grade school, Jas. As much as I wanna go off on you, I'm not even going to do it. You're not even worth it, and I got other shit to deal with that I would love to talk to my best friend about, but it's clear you ain't no kind of best friend. Fuck off my line, bitch."

Click

I hung up on her ass. I have no idea what she would have said after I told her that I knew about her plotting. But quite frankly, I don't even give a fuck. There's nothing she can say to justify being a terrible friend. As many niggas she done cheated on and as many bitches who niggas she done fucked on, I never once crossed her. So sorry, foul play is foul play, and I ain't too fond of second chances. Fuck me over once, you won't ever be able to fuck me over again. I don't care how deep we in this shit.

She kept blowing my phone up, and I kept sending her to voicemail. I finally pulled up into the driveway of my home and ran inside once I seen Wes had made it back home. When I walked in, he was sleeping like a baby, I damn near didn't want to disturb him.

I kicked his leg. "Wake the fuck up."

He jumped up like I woke him up out of a bad dream. "Baby, what's wrong?" He immediately checked his phone. "SHIT! I missed a call from the plug."

"Nigga, you missed a call from me. Fuck the plug. Who did you have kill Mike?"

He looked at me shocked.

"Baby, as much as I wanted that nigga dead, I ain't have nothing to do with that. I told you that might be

Karisma's biological father, and it's not even you to question my character."

I wouldn't be questioning him if he hadn't threatened Mike the other day to me. "Well I was just over there, and..."

"What the fuck you mean you was just over there? You fucking that nigga?" He cut me off and stood up.

"I went over there to tell him I was pregnant, and there's a possibility that the child might be his. After I left, he was shot. And if I was fucking him, I won't be able to fuck him again, so enough of you asking questions. I'm the one asking the questions now. Now who did you have kill him?"

"I just told you I was not involved with any of that. That nigga got more enemies than me, and what you mean he might be the father?"

"The same day me and you got together, that morning he had just bust in me after he pistol whipped me. I never brought it up because I didn't think it was important or even that I would end up pregnant."

He just got up, walked away and left out the house without saying anything to me. How could he even be mad? We didn't have any breaks between me and Mike breaking up and getting with him. And I never once slept with Mike since I been with Wes. I was close to doing it tonight, but that's not the point. I still had not slept with

Mike. I can't believe he so butt hurt over something that could have been prevented by him not busting in me like he even takes care of the one he has full time. He just instantly pissed me off acting like a child. I followed him to his car.

"Yeah, run like a little ass bitch ass boy!" I yelled behind him.

He turned around and choked me up. "Mica, I'll never beat yo ass like Mike did, but I will choke yo little ass up. I need some air; stop acting like a nut, and don't ever in your life call me another bitch."

"You the one acting like a little ass boy, walking away cause a conversation didn't go your way!"

"Mica, I said I need some air!" He yelled.

"Find out who killed Mike while you're out meditating and shit!" I yelled.

I know he had something to do with it. He just didn't want to admit it.

After Wes left out, I got back in the shower and headed to bed; I was exhausted. This baby makes a short day seem long. I'm ready for this pregnancy to be over with. Once again, Jas was blowing my phone up. What did she miss from she's not worth it? I have nothing to talk to her about. I picked up and stayed silent. She was sounding like she was running and screaming.

"Mica! Mica! Get out of the house right now!" I dropped my phone, ran to put my shoes on and grabbed my keys. When I opened the door, Nyla was standing right there. I just stopped and looked at her up and down.

"May I come in?" She asked.

I opened the door up. "No, you may not. Wes isn't here if you're looking for him," I said calmly.

"Nope, I'm here for you. I told you I wanted you to stay away from him. I said I want my man and my life back. So, since you didn't want to listen, I sent the message through Mike. Pack your bags and disappear. Hell, kill yourself. I don't give a fuck, just stay away from Wes and our daughter. If you do not listen, I'll make an example out of Jas next."

"He isn't your man, and Jas is his sister. You really think he'll forgive you? Karisma not even your goddamn child. He doesn't want anything to do with your dumbass. You're miserable. You can leave now," I said to her.

"Yeah, I'll leave, but I'll be back," she said turning around and leaving.

What is wrong with this bitch? Been out of jail one day and has a murder on her hands. I called Wes' cell phone. He didn't answer so I texted him. PLEASE COME HOME SOON!

Me and him need to talk about all this shit. I still haven't even had the chance to talk to him about my father. As mad as I am at Jas, I still wouldn't want her to get killed. Not over some shit that could have been avoided. But then again, that's what she gets for thinking that bitch was her friend.

****

Jas

I called Mica because I know Nyla was on some nut shit. When Nyla called me back, she said she didn't do anything, and she was on her way to see me. Me and Nyla been cool for years even tho she and my brother dated, me and her also had a thing on the low. I would consider Nyla the love of my life, but she doesn't even understand how much I love her yet. As many men I have been with, Nyla was the only person that could make me feel butterflies. Although she was fucking my brother, I still always felt like number one. We used to sit up day and night talking about everything, from our goals and inspirations down to the needy greedy drama and her and my brother's relationship. A part of me always felt bad for fucking on her while she was with my brother; she was my kryptonite. I could barely breath in a good way around her. I wanted her to suffocate me in her presence. I still catch myself daydreaming about the first hook up between her and I.

Nyla and my brother just got done having a bad fight, so she asked to move in with me for a few days because they needed a break. I ain't think nothing of it. Nyla don't have no family, so I wasn't just gone have her out here bad. I have a two bedroom, so her living with me was no problem. She came over crying about the altercation that happened earlier between her and Wes. I poured up some wine and just listened to her vent. That's when I realized how beautiful she was. Literally stunning. I'd say her best feature is her lips; they were so juicy, big and like a deep dark pinkish color. On her brown skin, those lips are to die for. After she got done pouring her heart out about Wes, she grabbed the bottle of wine that was now empty and frowned.

"We need something stronger," she said.

"I don't drink hard liquor, but I got some patron in the kitchen if you'd like."

"You gone make me drink by myself?"

"I'll have a beer."

I went to the kitchen to grab the patron for her, and myself a beer. We were watching music videos on BET and Nyla got up and started dancing. The way she was moving her body made me want to drown between her thighs, and I had never even been with another woman before. All the years me and Mica been together, I never looked at her this way, so I can't even believe these thoughts we're running through my mind.

"Come on dance with me," Nyla said, grabbing my hand for me to stand up.

"I don't see nothing wrong with a lil bump n grind." R Kelly blasted through my TV, speakers. Every time Nyla moved her hips on my body, it made me get wetter. I started holding her hips harder, digging into her leggings. She then turned around.

"Ever been with a woman before, Jas?"

"Nah," I said.

Nyla than started kissing me. Her lips were so big and juicy, I couldn't help but to bite her bottom lip. She pushed me on top of the couch and straddled me. The moment felt like a lesbian scene you would see in a movie. We were breathing hard and kissing hard. I lifted her shirt up and started kissing her chest. Unstrapping her bra, I went down to suck on her nipples. This was my first time doing any of this, but it all came so naturally. Nyla got off my lap and got on her knees. I had a short lil blue dress on with no panties. I never wear panties. She opened my legs and started blowing on my clit. I put my head back and moaned loud. I was far from drunk, so I know the liquor wasn't the reason I was doing this. She just made me feel some type of way.

The first time her tongue touched my clit, it literally felt like nothing I have ever felt before. I've had my pussy eaten by a handful of men before, but the way she did it was like she knew exactly how to please me. I wanted to taste her too. I got up and laid her flat on the ground and went down on her. She tasted amazing, and she's a creamer. While I was licking her clit, I put two fingers inside her pussy and rubbed the roof of it. She was screaming and shaking yelling "Don't stop!" I wasn't gone stop even if she wanted me too. A few more strokes inside her pussy with my fingers and she exploded all over them, leaving my fingers drenched in her juices.

"Lemme taste it, baby."

I put my fingers to her lips, and she sucked everything she left on them off. We cuddled and fell asleep right on the floor.

Ever since then, Nyla and I been fucking around, and that was two years ago. She was giving me more pussy than she was giving Wes. She always complained about how he didn't know how to please her the way I did. I took it as a compliment but at the same time wondered why she just didn't leave him for me.

Knock Knock

I went to open the door and it was Nyla. She walked in and started kissing me. It was out of nowhere, and I know she was just mad at me. But her lips on mine seemed so right. I kissed her back. I started to stumble down to the couch in my living room and she hopped on top of me, just like she did the first time we fucked.

"Why you are playing with me, Nyla," I said in a 'stop, no don't stop' type of way.

"You know I love you, just let it happen."

She choked my neck and put her fingers in my mouth. Then she started kissing me again and slid two fingers under my skirt. I gasped for air. She always knew how to touch me to get me going. I started kissing on her neck while she was on top of me. I trailed my tongue from her neck down to her nipples. She has the prettiest nipples I've ever seen. I sucked on them real soft because that's how she liked it. She sucked on mine with more aggression because she knew that's how I liked it. She started moving her fingers fast around my clitoris and I came all over her fingers. I wouldn't leave her hanging so I slid my fingers in her shorts and she was soaking wet. Like dripping. She was moaning loud. I knew when she got loud she was ready to explode. So, I kept going faster. Sure enough, she started to scream, which means she came. I took my fingers out her pants, put them in her mouth and made her suck her own pussy juices. We started to kiss when she got up and buckled her shorts back up. She went to the purse she dropped on the floor, and I went to grab us a glass of water.

When I came back, she was holding a gun towards me. "I just had to see if the sex was the same, and it is. But the loyalty is not."

Wes opened the door and before she could turn around, "BOOM!"

He killed her. She was going to kill me. So much for the best nipples and best sex I've ever had. Now how am I gone explain this mess to my brother?

Chapter 7

Mica

Wes finally came home with blood all over him. He walked in stumbling and crying. I grabbed him.

"Baby, what's wrong?" I said.

"I had to kill Nyla. She tried to kill Jas. She was going to kill my sister... I had to... had to. Fuck!"

Eh, I wasn't mad. Why is he crying? He was rambling on and on. Somebody had to go. Did he want it to be me, him, or Jas. He got up and went in the shower. I called Jas's phone.

"Girl, are you ok?" Although she been a terrible friend, I still wanna check up on her and make sure she good. I don't know what I'd do if she died.

"Yeah, I'm good. I'm sorry for being a messy ass friend," she said.

"Girl, you good. You know I love you. Rest up and I'll call you later."

I hung up.

I waited for Wes to come back in the room, so I could help him unwind. I grabbed my phone and went back to google. The first thing that popped up was my father's death again. I instantly got pissed, but I stayed calm.

Wes came out the shower and laid on the bed naked. I gave him that look like I wanted so bad to taste him. I started to give him brain. He was hesitant at first, which I understood. He just got done blowing the brains of his baby mother out. I looked up at him and asked him to play a freaky game.

He said, "Shit. Baby, too much been happening today. I really just wanna call it a night and go to sleep." I grabbed the handcuffs out my drawer and handcuffed him to the bed.

"Baby, you know you accountable for everything you do, right?"

He nodded his head *yes* in a clearly confused way.

"And you should watch what you say cause that shit might come back to you, right?" I said, tracing his dick with my finger.

He nodded his head again. Then I got up and grabbed his gun out the side of his dresser.

I cocked it back, looked at him and smiled. "That nigga you killed because you owed him some work was my daddy, bitch."

POW!

****

7 months later

"I don't want Chipotle. I want Qdoba!" I yelled at Wes. I'm pregnant as hell and he's trying to tell me what I want to eat. Like he's the one with the cravings, and I just have this big ass stomach attached to me. I know you were probably thinking I killed him. Nope. I shot at him, but I didn't shoot him. I'm just as shocked as you are that he's still with me. After shooting at him, Wes has removed all weapons from the house, and I think he sleeps with one eye open now. I don't blame him. I've become a little crazy these days.

We pulled up in Qdoba and the line was long as hell. There was no way that my big ass was going to stand in line. "I want a steak burrito bowl, extra steak, queso, habanero sauce, cheese and extra sour cream with chips on the side," I said without even breathing.

My mouth watered even thinking about the food. I was desperately hungry for a burrito bowl. I've been coming to Qdoba since the day they opened, and every time I come, I get the same exact thing. When Wes got out the car, I had two missed calls from a number I never seen before. They didn't leave a voicemail, so it must not be important.

Life has been great for me these days. I'm 8 months pregnant and this baby is damn near about to get evicted. I'm tired of being pregnant. Wes has been amazing to me and despite all the ups and downs; we managed to get through it all. Not to mention he proposed to me a few weeks ago. I'm ecstatic. We agreed that we will have the wedding after I have the baby because my idea of getting married is not being blown up and wobbling. I can't wait to drop this baby and finally go dress shopping and stuff. We aren't wasting anytime; as soon as my body snap back, it's going to be wedding planning time.

Nyla and Cynthia are no longer in our lives, so we shouldn't have to worry about anyone objecting to us getting married. We also agreed to no more killing. I promised him I wouldn't body another bitch. If I feel like I need to, I promised Wes I'd run it by him first. Especially since Mike not here to help me cover my tracks. I may have lied but let's just hope no one crossed me. I ain't heard from Mike or anything about the situation since the last time I seen him; everyone just assumed he must be dead. It's been 7 months since all that shit went down and honestly, the past 6 months have been amazing without all the extra drama and bullshit.

That unknown number called me again. I ignored it. Wes finally got back to the car and we drove home. After I finished eating, Wes started rubbing on me. I haven't been a big fan of sex lately because of the baby; I just feel so damn gigantic. I told him to stop, then he whispered in my ear.

"You're going to be my wife soon. You think this is the worst I'm going to see you?" We both laughed. He is always trying to make a joke bout of something. "Plus, this what you gone do with the next baby?"

Wes has been saying after this one he wants to have another one because we are having a girl, and he badly wants a boy. But little does he know, until my baby girl is at least 5, he not having another one. I got up out the bed.

"I'm getting my tubes tied," I laughed. I ran to the bathroom and locked the door. He chased after me and started banging on the doors.

"You not even old enough to get your tubes tied," he laughed.

"BIRTH CONTROL!" I yelled then turned the shower on.

If I end up pregnant again, I wouldn't mind it. Wes is an amazing man, I just wanna adjust to the first one before I start planning on a second one. Plus, in a couple weeks, Wes will have full custody of Karisma. I don't think he understands how busy our lives are about to get with two kids.

Once again, I'm getting a call from this unknown number. I picked up but kept quiet.

"Damn, you finally picked up."

My mouth dropped. It was Mike! I couldn't believe my ears. I thought he was dead, it has been 7 months of thinking he died.

"What... I thought you were dead," I said as I started to cry.

"They can't kill me off that easily."

"I can't talk right now, I'll call you back later" I said then hung up

I was lost for words; this was all way too much to handle. What is he going to think about me and Wes being engaged? Now I'm back to having two baby daddies. I got in the shower and washed up quick then walked to the bedroom.

"Wes, we need to get blood work done to find out if this is your baby."

He started getting uptight. "MICA, THATS MY BABY REGARDLESS!" He yelled.

I loved the fact that he's a standup guy but let's be honest, he's gonna have to deal with Mike being around because Mike isn't going to the walk out and away on his child just because another nigga wishes to be the father. I wouldn't even expect that from Mike. I understand Wes's frustration though. Karisma might be Mike's child as well. He just wants something of his own. I can't blame him.

"Why you are bringing this shit up? The fuck wrong with you, Mica?"

"Mike isn't dead," I said while biting my lip.

"What do you mean he ain't dead?" Wes asked.

I didn't know how to answer that because it's all shocking to me, but the man I heard on the phone was for sure Mike.

"He called me while I was in the bathroom. I know I said he was dead because I saw him lying on the ground shot. We hadn't heard anything about a funeral or anything. Before you killed Nyla, she came over to the house and threatened me to leave you alone. She said she made an example out of Mike, so I figured he was dead."

For the rest of the day, me and Wes caked up in the house enjoying one another's company. He always knew how to make a strange situation good, and that's why I love him so much. I've never felt this way about anyone, not even Mike and the seven years we spent together. I know for a fact that even though Wes says if this baby isn't his he still going to be there, he would still have doubts and I would too. I would want to raise my child in the same household as the father. Mike has changed and been a good man; of course, before he rose from the dead.

I fell asleep with my head on Wes' lap while we were watching a movie. When I woke up Wes was gone, and a blanket was covering me. I walked to the kitchen to grab something to drink and there was a sticky note on the fridge: *'I knew your thirsty cute ass was gone come in here first. Baby, I ran to the store. I love you."*

That little sticky note lit up my world he knows me so well. It was 7 at night, and I forgot I had a nail appointment for 6:45. I called the shop and told my nail tech Tasha I had fallen asleep.

"Girl, bring your pregnant ass on," she laughed.

When I got to the shop, I sat right in Tasha's booth. She was finishing up on another client and then came to me.

"Girl, how the fuck you been? And you getting so big. Oh my God," she said while trying to rub my stomach.

"I been good, just living, enjoying life and trying to have a healthy baby."

"Girl, I'm surprised you pregnant. Remember in middle school you said you wasn't having kids till you 40?" We both started cracking up laughing.

"Now look at me," I said, smiling while looking at my stomach.

Being a mother scared me and it still does. I know I'll be just fine though because I know for a fact I never want to be the kind of mother that my mother was. She was always in and out of my life and always chose niggas over me. It was sad. Saddest part is I had to be raised by the foster system because her and my father both failed me.

While Tasha was doing my nails, I could hear the two ladies in the booth talking about a situation that don't have shit to do with them.

"Girl, you know that nigga Mike from off Halsted? I heard he got shot months ago and people thought he was dead. Now suddenly he's back," one of the nosey ass bitches said.

"Yeah, I heard Wes did it. He need to be in jail. That nigga always killing somebody."

"Wes ain't shoot nobody, and you bitches need to mind yawl business," I said.

They both rolled their eyes at me and continued with the conversation.

"Girl, I don't know why you pay any of these gossiping bitches any attention," Tasha whispered.

Chapter 8

Mike

It has been seven months since I have heard Mica's voice. She sounded so happy and at peace. Who am I to try and take that from her? Despite everything I have ever done to her, she knows I love her, and I would never want to take her happiness away. But let's be honest. If you have ever had to watch the person you love, love someone else, you could understand that when that feeling hits, it always hits hard. You can literally feel that pain in your chest.

I was in the hospital for three months since the day I got shot at; the bullet grazed my head and I lost a lot of blood. They had me hooked up to all kinds of weird ass machines that did all kinds of different stuff. Everyday being there, I wondered how Mica was doing, and if the baby was growing healthy. I was having dreams that Mica, myself and the baby had a chance at being a family. It made my body cringe at the thought of the baby even possibly being Wes's because me knowing Mica and how loyal she is, there would never be another chance for her and I.

The first week I was let out of the hospital, I found myself steady driving around her house and places I thought she would be. I went over in my head what I would say to her or how I would even explain all this. But I didn't want to interrupt her life and have her come to my rescue. The homie Sean and I came up on a decent amount of money and went to Jamaica for a while. It was a breath of fresh air to get away from Chicago. People were really trying their hardest to take my life. The night I got shot, I got out of Mica's car and tried to head into the house. Soon as Mica pulled off, Nyla came from behind the bushes and shot me three times; twice in my shoulder and once in the leg.

Ever since I called Mica, she been on my mental heavy, so I decided to call her.

Ring Ring Ring

I waited for her to pick the phone up. "Hey creep," I heard her saying on the other end.

I could tell from the sound of her voice that she was smiling. I didn't want to start an argument, so I'm not even going to bother asking her where she got that dumb ass creep shit. It sounds like some shit that nigga Wes would say. I swear I can't stand this nigga; he done already got down on me twice. If he thinks I ain't see him in the car waiting on Nyla when she shot me, he has another thing coming. I'm not even going to bother telling Mica because it's not even worth it. Plus, Wes gone get his sooner than expected, and I'm gone hit him where it's gone hurt.

The plus side of having a girl that's fucking the enemy is that they pillow talk so damn much. When I was fucking on Cynthia, she told me everything, and I mean everything. Even the shit about Wes killing Mica's father, Leroy. How can she forgive that nigga like nothing even happened, yet I'm damn near in the dog bed? Damn near dying because of my love for her. I'd rather be between her legs.

Mica and I always had amazing sex. The thought of me even touching her soft skin made my dick get rock hard. She always smelt amazing. I was picturing her in my head. Imagining her soft caramel skin. Her thick full lips and beautiful natural hair. It was at this very moment that I realized that I lost a queen. And at this very moment that I made a promise to myself that I would do everything in my power to try to get her back. I know I had my work cut out for me, but I can't breathe without Mica. I need her in my life.

****

Mica

"Man, how you been?" Mike said.

I smiled and responded, "I been good. Already eight months pregnant and ready to explode."

He laughed. I missed his laugh. "Girl, I missed you."

"Missed me so much that you didn't reach out and let me know you alive." I got so mad that quick and kept on talking. "Do you know how sad I was when I thought you died? How could you not reach out to me? Now you suddenly rose from the dead and back to interrupt my life once things got back calm and good?" I said without taking a breath and talking at 100 mph.

"It's not even like that, Mica. I had to get myself together. Plus, you already know I don't like to feel vulnerable. You know you pregnant, and I still don't know if it's my baby, so what you gone do? Shoot the muthafucka that shot me?" He said in a sarcastic ass way.

He knows I would. I don't even know why he asked that question.

"Damn right," I said, laughing.

"You a nut case, shorty."

"You love my nut ass, nigga, but let's get up tomorrow for lunch or something," I said.

"Alright, that's a bet. Let me call you back later, baby girl," he said.

Click.

He hung up quick as fuck. I wonder what he was in a rush to do. To be honest, its none of my business; he's not my man anymore. He can hang up on me for any reason, and it shouldn't be my concern. I should have asked him how Nyla was moving when she shot him. But like Wes said, I need to stop sweating that shit. His situation was beyond critical. Yet, I still need to know.

I got up to go make something to eat and right then and there, my water broke. I started to freak out. This shouldn't be happening. I'm only eight months. I have a little while before I'm supposed to go into labor.

I called Wes' phone and he picked up super quick. "Wassup creep," he said.

"Baby, my water just broke."

"Okay, stay calm and pack a lil bag. I'm on my way," he said then hung up.

Wassup with niggas hanging up so quick today. I only waited 10 minutes before Wes pulled up. He ran into the house, grabbed my bag and opened it up.

"WHAT THE HELL ARE YOU DOING, WES? I DONT NEED A BAG CHECK. WE HAVE TO GO!" I yelled.

He ignored me, went in our room and came back with a hand full of his things.

"If you think I ain't staying by your side for however long they plan on keeping you, you're crazy," he said.

He kissed me on my forehead, grabbed my hand and said, "Now let's go push our baby out."

I felt so much better. What did I do to deserve a man like Wes? He's literally everything I need and more. We walked to the car. Wes helped me get into the passenger seat. And just like that, we were off to go have the baby, still not knowing who the father is. Part of me still wished Mike could have been here. I feel bad letting Wes experience this moment when there's an chance that this child is not even his.

I have been in labor for seven hours so far; this baby is so damn stubborn. I'm for sure not having another baby no time soon. This pain is awful.

"Push, baby push!"

I pushed a little harder and my baby girl was here. The doctor handed me my baby and me and Wes both had tears in our eyes. I can't believe she is finally here.

"Excuse me, ma'am. Can we run a DNA test right now?" I asked.

I looked at Wes and his mouth dropped to the floor.

"Yeah, of course," the doctor said. She left out the room and me and Wes were both quiet. She came back and did a mouth swab on him and the baby.

"Now that I have that, lets fill out the birth certificate form. What would you like to name the beautiful baby?"

"I would like to wait for the DNA results before I do that, ma'am."

"That could take up to 3 days."

"That's fine since we will be here anyways."

The doctor walked out of the room and Wes just looked at me confused.

"You can't possibly think it's okay putting your name on my baby's birth certificate without finding out if you are even the father. Don't give me that look. This is the right thing to do," I said.

"That's wild, Mica. If that nigga Mike never popped back up, you wouldn't be saying all this shit, but aight," he said, heated.

"No, I prob wouldn't, but the fact of the matter is he is. Right is right and wrong is wrong. I'm not saying I'm going to leave you for him. All I'm saying is he has a right to know if this is his baby. Just like you have a baby with Nyla and I deal with it, if it was Mike's baby, you're going to have to deal with it to, baby," I said, almost crying.

"Yeah, you right, creep. I'm tripping. I'm sorry. I love you." He kissed me on my forehead.

"I love you too, creep," I said with a big ass smile on my face.

****

Wes

I cannot believe Mica doing this right now. I know I said I'm tripping, but this shit is crazy. I been by her side though this entire situation. I helped her out of that fucked up situation she was in with Mike before we got together. Even if this baby is his, he does not deserve to be in the baby life. I don't care what Mica say, that's my fucking baby. End of discussion. I see getting Mike popped didn't teach him a lesson to never cross me again. I'm gone pay this nigga a visit and make sure he understands loud and clear that I'm not to be fucked with. I can't wait till Mica get healed up, so we can have gone ahead and get married. Then we can put this nigga behind us for good. She better make it known she happy when those results come back that the baby is mine; talking about she doesn't know what she gone name her. My name Wes, and my daughter name gone be Whitney.

Mica was sleep, so I started remembering back to the day Nyla shot Mike.

I called her up about the bullshit Mica said her and Jas pulled in the club. I wanted to talk in person, so we were driving around the city talking about all the shit that been happening in our lives. I told her about how much Mike been a problem for me, and although Nyla used to fuck on him, she still wasn't a fan of him. He used to beat her ass how he beat on Mica; that's another reason why I ain't fuck with him.

"So, what you wanna do about it? You wanna cry like a bitch or kill this nigga?"

"Man, only reason I ain't have this nigga put six feet under is because of the fact he used to fuck with Cynthia and Karisma might be his daughter."

"But she's not his daughter. Who been around all 5 years of her life? Even if he was, DNA don't make a nigga a father."

"I ain't the type to have blood on my hands," I said.

"Well let me do it."

We drove over to Mike's crib, and I parked my car a block away. Nyla got out the car and walked to the crib. Took her ass forever to get back. When I asked her what took so long, she said the nigga was in the car talking to a bitch. She handled the business, said she was sure he was dead, and I took her back to her car, so we went separate ways.

I busted a few moves to make a couple dollars, and in the process, Nyla had left me to go fuck with my girl and try to kill my sister. Just the thought of the fact that she was on that makes my ass itch. I thought we were better than that. I knew Nyla was with the shits, but I never thought she would take it that damn far.

I needed to go for a little drive and clear my head. Too much was on my mind. I stopped at the gas station down the street from the lake to get some black and mild's. I planned on sitting by the water and tryna understand when and where my life became so hectic. Seems like it all started when I got with Mica. I'm not blaming her for all this mess, but shit was cool and smooth before I tried to save her. I walked into the store and it was damn near empty. I seen one person with some type of pink hair. I kept walking to the register.

"Wes, is that you?" The familiar voice said. The woman behind me was Ashley.

"Man Ashley, what you are doing in town, bruh?" I said, smiling.

I hadn't seen Ashley in four years. We never dated because I just wanted to fuck at the time. Her, on the other hand… she wanted to cuff a nigga up, own homes, have kids, the whole nine yards. At the time, I was not ready for all of that. If only I was smart enough, my life would be so different. I was young minded when I first met her. All I wanted to do was get in some pussy, make my money and take care of my daughter.

"Well I don't know if you know, but my mother passed a few days ago. I'm here to bury her, then I'm heading back to LA," she said.

"Awe man, I'm sorry for your loss. Where the funeral going to be at? You know miss Parks always looked out for me. I gotta make sure I show my respects."

"Angle Crest Funeral Homes over there on Halsted. But what you about to do? Its late, you need to be at home," she said, laughing.

"I'm just out and about trying to clear my head, that's all."

"Well can I be out and about with you? We have a lot of catching up to do."

"Lemme buy these filter tips really quick. I'm only going up the street to the water. You can join me."

"Damn boy! You still smoking those things?"

We both laughed. I must admit, four years ago, Ashley was fine as hell. But at this very moment, she looked so beautiful and even better than the last time I seen her. Ashley is black and Dominican. she has long curly hair and a body you only see on TV. She could be one of them hoes on basketball wives, just with a better face. I love Mica, so I don't plan on doing anything stupid. Still, having someone to vent to with everything I got going on that won't judge me, that's exactly something I need right now.

"Aight, you ready?"

"You take the lead, creep."

She's the one that got me hooked on saying creep. I wish she would have never said it. Our past just hit me like a ton of bricks. Damn, I missed this girl.

Chapter 9

Wes

It was midnight, and instead of being next to the woman I love that just gave birth to our child, I was out by the water with a woman I could have loved many years ago.

"So, go ahead and catch me up, Creep," I said to Ashley.

"So, besides the fact my mother just passed... I have a two-year-old son now; his daddy ain't shit. Well, he doesn't even know he's his son because I don't want him in my life. I have been working on my fashion company in LA. Things been going good with that. Besides that, ain't nothing interesting been happening to me," she said without slowing down.

"Well, what's your son's name, and where the father at?"

"His name Mikehale, and he lives here," she said.

I stopped asking questions because I could tell the topic was a touchy topic for her. I pulled her closer to me because I knew she needed to be held. It was innocent of course. But nobody should have to go through what she's going through, especially raising a child alone. I wouldn't wish that on my worst enemy.

"Remember when we were out here four years ago?" She said, smiling.

"Yeah, we fucked somewhere on this lake." We both cracked up.

Those were the good ole days. Ashley always been spontaneous, and we always had fun together no matter what. We could be at a funeral home and her ass would be trying to get kicked down. We fucked anywhere we could fuck.

"I missed you cre-"

I cut her off and placed my lips on hers. I had to taste her and see if that feeling was still there. And just like I imagined, the feeling was still there. For a second, I forgot all about Mica.

****

Ashley

Did that just really happen? Did this man just kiss me? I wanted this kiss. I needed this kiss, but both our lives are too complicated, even though I still don't know what's even going on in his.

"What was that for?" I asked.

"I regret not taking you serious years ago, but I needed to see if that vibe was still there; I haven't felt that feeling since you. There's no way that me and you could be anything more than friends. My girl just had our baby, and I love her. However, I'm also not willing to let you go yet. I want to spend as much time as possible with you until you leave," he said.

Talk about laying it on me heavy. He did just that; I was lost for words. I wanted to give Wes the world years ago, not that he ain't already have everything he needed and more. I just wanted to add to it. I had the dreams of big homes, kids, vacations, etc. All of that was too much for him. He was not ready to grow up or commit. At least not to me. I think he still thinks I ain't know about him and Nyla. He kept telling me he wasn't ready for a relationship and just focusing on his daughter when the whole time he was in a relationship with her.

"So, what are we going to do?" I asked, confused.

I hope he didn't expect me to be a side bitch. That's not me, and he knows I deserve more than that. I'm beautiful with my head on my shoulders and my life together. He couldn't find another me if he tried. Not to toot my own horn, but in the humblest way possible, I'm the shit and play second to nobody. Especially when I got niggas out here trying to eat my ass like a pink starburst.

"I mean, let's just chill and see where things go," he said.

Things can either go good or bad, but I love Wes and always have, so whatever his plan was I was willing to go along with it if it don't involve hiding out and sneaking. I'll be in Chicago a few more weeks planning my mother's funeral, and then I'm gone. I'll be damned if I move back here, so unless we want to try that long-distance shit, I ain't the woman for the job.

"How about we go to my hotel room?" I said while kissing him on his lips. As much of a bad idea this all is, I'm dying to feel him deep in me.

****

Wes

"Baby, how you feeling? Are you good?" I said through the phone.

"Yeah. When are you coming back?" Mica asked.

"Give me a few more hours, baby."

I just did what I never wanted to do and that was lie and hide things from Mica. I wouldn't expect her to understand these feelings that came to me just by seeing Ashley's face. I walked back into the room with Ashley, and she was laying on the bed in a tank top and shorts. At that moment, all my worries about Mica had went away. Once again, I had forgotten all about Mica.

"So, I take it you don't plan on staying the night with me, " Ashley said, smiling.

"I would love to, I just can't. She just had the baby and at the hospital by herself...."

She cut me off and kissed me; it felt so good. It was so wrong but felt oddly like the right thing to do. She got up, laid me on my back and sat on me whiling kissing me harder and grinding her pussy against my sweats. I know she can tell she woke a monster up. I was hard as a rock.

"As much as I want to fuck the shit out of you, Wes, we both know we can't afford to do it. We both have good things going for us. I will always love you, but imma need for you to get up, and at least pretend she's the one you want to be with because she needs you right now. I can wait for you. Its already been four years."

The way she said all that was smooth as fuck and so mature in my eyes. It made me want her more. Everything she was saying was facts. Mica doesn't deserve this. If only Ashley knew how crazy Mica was, she would not even be here with me. Fucking around with me, she'll end up in whatever hole Cynthia in.

"Aight, hit my line soon before you disappear," I said after placing a kiss on her forehead.

Chapter 10

Mica

I've been sitting in this hospital room by myself for hours. Wes just went ghost. I just gave birth to my precious little girl and the man that wants to be father the most just up and left. I called Mike. Not because I want to cause problems but because if this is his daughter, he deserves to know. Not only that, I'm feeling mad alone at the time I need company the most.

"Hello," he said after the first ring.

"I thought I should call you and let you know that I gave birth. It was a bit early, but she is 100% healthy," I said with a smile on my face.

Mike was quiet for a long pause. When he finally began to speak again, I could hear the crack in his voice and knew he was crying.

"Awe man, I know she's beautiful too."

"Would you like to come see her?" I asked.

"Hell yeah, I'm on my way right now."

Click.

That phone call really made me smile and laugh. He was so eager to hear me ask him to come see his possible daughter. I'm beyond proud of Mike's growth. He has come a long way from the piece of shit he once was. I guess it's true what they say. Some people just never know what they had until its gone. In Mike's case, what he had was a family. If this baby is not Wes', Mike may miss out on many moments with his daughter. Wes has made it clear that regardless he was going to be the father through DNA or without it, even though he chose not to be here with me right now.

I don't even know exactly what I'm going to do when I find out who's the father. If I should stay with Wes, and coparent with Mike. Or just leave both alone and raise my daughter by myself. Plenty women do it every day, but why would I do it by choice? Mike was not always a terrible person. He was once sweet and kind and that's why I fell for him in the first place. It wasn't until towards the end of our relationship that he started being abusive towards me. He cheated a few times but the last girl I caught him up with, I felt like he was in love with her and it wasn't Cynthia. I don't even know the girl's name but if I seen her face, I would know her for sure. A few years back, Jas showed me pictures from Instagram of Mike hugged up with her. I had confronted him about it and he beat my ass. Afterwards, he promised to never see her again. That was the last time we ever spoke of the situation.

It's now going on 5 in the morning, and Wes still hasn't showed up. I asked the nurse to bring my baby back in the room with me, so she could sleep next to me. I waited until she fell asleep before I tried to get any sleep. She looked so peaceful like she didn't have any worries in the world. It warmed my heart to know that she came from me. My flesh and blood.

****

Wes

Time started to fly spending it with Ashley. Ashley looks even more beautiful than she was the last time I had seen her. Her soft brown skin melts me every time. She has always been stunning. I know I got Mica already, and I would never intentionally try to hurt her, but I can't pretend like there isn't a spark between Ashley and me. I was driving back to the hospital when I decided to stop and get Mica some flowers. She had just given birth to my baby girl while I'm out here making her look stupid and locking tongues with Ashley. I got my baby some roses because she loves them and a box of chocolate since she been craving chocolate like crazy her entire pregnancy. It was 8 am when I finally made it back to the hospital.

"Where's my sexy mamma?" I said, walking into her room holding the flowers and chocolate. Only to find her laying on the bed watching Mike sit on the chair holding our daughter. "What the fuck going on in here? Why the fuck is he even here, Mica?" She looked at me like she was lost for words and didn't know what to say.

"Baby, he just here to see her for a little while," she said.

"Exactly, that's what I'm not understanding. Why does he need to see our child?"

"Man, stop playing the fuck out of crazy, Wes. You know damn well there's a possibility of her being my child. I have never disrespected you before, and I don't plan on doing it now. Mica called me and asked me to come, so I'm here."

This nigga got a thing for being the father to the kids that are supposed to be mine or fucking on what's mine. I'm starting to get sick of his ass.

****

Mike

I can't believe this nigga in here acting like a bitch, crying and whining because Mica allowed me to see the child that I'm 100% sure is mine. I just need him to move around and let me have back what has always been mine. I told Mica I was going to leave to go get something to eat. Right when I got to Wendy's, my phone started to ring.

"Hello," I answered.

"Hey creep, grab me a four for four. The nurses aren't feeding me right."

"Nah, you just greedy, girl."

We both laughed.

"Aight, I'll see you in a little, baby."

Click.

When I got back to the room, Mica was sitting on her bed holding our daughter, and Wes's ass was in the chair staring at me like he wanted to rip my head off my shoulders. Good thing the nurse walked in to ease the tension in the room.

"Mica, we got the DNA results faster than we planned."

She handed Mica the results and Wes and I looked at her hand, waiting for her to open them. She just kept staring at the envelope.

"Mica, open that shit, so we can dead all this bullshit," I said.

She opened the envelope and started crying. "Wes, you're not the father, baby."

Wes started screaming and hollering like the bitch he is, punching shit and left out the room. Wes not the father so we knew for a fact that I was. I understand they planned on having a family, and this picture-perfect idea of how they thought shit was gone go. Now they gotta add me in the picture because I don't plan on leaving my daughter's side. This is my first child and I can't wait to right my wrongs. Next step gets her out that crib and back home with me. I'll be damned if she thinks they about to play house with my daughter.

****

Wes

That shit just blew me. I'm hurt and pissed off at the same time. I wanna rip that nigga head apart. How he nuts in her one time, I nut in her our whole relationship, and the baby end up being his. I cried all the way back to the Holiday Inn to Ashley's room. When she answered the door, her hair was put up in a ponytail, and she had a robe on. I grabbed her and threw her on the bed. I was about to take my frustration out on her pussy.

"Wes, what are you doing? Are you sure you want to do this?" She asked.

I ignored her, skipped all the foreplay, no kissing, no fingers, no licking, none of that shit. I spat on my dick, pulled her panties to the side and stuck my raw dick inside of her. In all honesty, I wasn't even paying Ashley no attention. In my mind I was picturing Mica. I was choking her and pulling her hair. I left my hand print on her ass.

"You like this rough shit, don't you? This what you like, huh?" I said while fucking Ashley harder.

"Yes! Yes! Yes!" Ashley screamed.

"That's supposed to be my baby, bitch," I said.

I have never called any woman a bitch, but it's the truth. That was supposed to be my baby. Ashley realized what I said and pushed me off her.

"Who was supposed to be your baby? Were you seriously thinking about your baby momma while in me? The child not yours?"

I just looked at her and walked out the room, not in the mood to pillow talk. I just took all my anger out on poor Ashley, but it really did make me feel a lot better.

****

Mica

I am lost for words, speechless and confused. Although I knew there was a chance of Mike being the father, I didn't think it would happen. I also didn't expect Wes to run out on me the way that he did. He told me that no matter what, we were going to figure this out. Before we can, he done already gave up and lost hope. Mike has yet to leave my side. The person I least expected to be here the most is outshining the man I love.

"You know we gone be okay, right Mica?"

"Yeah, I know, but what about Wes and me?" I said.

"He a grown man. I can't tell him how to move. All I can do is show you and treat you how you should be treated and be the best father I can possibly be."

Everything Mike was saying was deep and the truth. I've been fighting everything that's been running in my head and what if God sent him back into my life for a reason. What if Wes not the one for me? While all of this continued to run through my mind, the doctor came into the room to let me know they would be discharging me later this afternoon. I don't even know what to do. Go back to the home me and Wes share? A hotel? I'm sure Wes wants nothing else to do with me. He talked all this bullshit about being the father no matter what and now when shit gets real, he's nowhere to be found. For the rest of my time in the hospital, me and Mike talked about everything, from what type of parents we're going to be, to what she can and cannot wear on the day of her high school prom.

"So, what we going to name her?" Mike asked.

"Whitney Wiley," I said.

It's the name I would have given her if she was still Wes's child. Although she's not, she's still going to be his daughter. He was there with me through the entire 9 months. It's not going to be that easy for him to just walk out on her and I like this. We can still find a happy medium with Mike in the picture. We've overcome so much more, this is legit light work. That's why my daughter has his last name. We will be together forever. Plus, we are still getting married soon.

****

Mike

Although Mica didn't just come out and say she named my daughter Whitney because that nigga name is Wes, I'm already knowing that's the reason behind it. I'll be damned if she thinks they about to play house with my daughter. It kills my soul knowing that I fucked our situation up, not knowing how to be a man. I will get Mica back. I don't care if it takes my own blood, sweat and tears. I need her; she has been the only reason for me living for years. It still angers me the way she just up and dipped on me.

Wes had walked out on Mica and never returned. it was now time for her to be discharged and she kept calling that nigga's phone for it to constantly go to voicemail. I finally got sick of looking at the desperation on her face.

"Aye, I'll take yawl to the crib. I don't know why you are acting like I'm not standing here."

She didn't respond, just kept staring at me. All her things were packed, so I put her bags on my shoulders, grabbed Whitney's car seat and we headed out the hospital.

The entire ride to her crib, she kept calling his phone and still no answer. When we finally got to the house, Wes' car was parked outside. Mica and I both looked at one another confused because if he been home this entire time, why hasn't he responded to her? I tried to get out the car to help her with her things.

"I think its best if you stay here, Mike."

She grabbed all of her and Whitney's bags and sat them in front of the house door, then came back and grabbed Whitney. Before closing the door, she looked at me for a second with a blank stare as if she had something she wanted to say to me.

"You can go," she said with a tear falling from her cheek.

I did just that, I left. Not because I wanted to, but because it was her wishes. If only Mica could see that Wes is the man that wants her. I am the man that needs her and will try my hardest to maintain the bond we have built again after I destroyed the previous one.

Chapter 11

Wes

I knew Mica had been calling my phone. I knew there was things her and I needed to talk about. I couldn't bring myself to even face her after what I did with Ashley. Between Mica and Ashley, my phone is as good as dead. They both won't stop calling me. I understand Mica's side. I walked out on her without talking or giving her the respect of being a man of my word. She's my woman, and I made her feel less. Ashley, on the other hand, was a much-needed fuck to let go of built up anger I had inside. Did it feel good? Of course. But her sex is nothing compared to the headboard banging love making moments Mica and I have.

I watched Mica get out of Mike's car. I can't blame her. I wasn't responding to her. How else was she supposed to get home? Her car been parked in the garage since the day she went into labor. A part of me beats myself up inside because I'm giving him the opportunity to get close to her again. Knowing Mica and all he put her through, I doubt she would take the bait.

When Mica walked inside the door with the baby, she said nothing to me, kept walking to the baby's room and left the other bags on the porch. I grabbed the other bags. Whitney was asleep, so she put her in the crib we bought her a couple weeks ago. We decorated her room pink with white dots all over the wall. She has fluffy white rugs all over her room and tons of toys and stuffed animals to play with. Mica walked out of the room with the baby monitor in one hand, and still did not say a word to me. The vibes she was giving me was like she had already known about what I did with Ashley. Thinking clearly, I knew that was impossible, so I kept my cool. On her way to the kitchen, I grabbed her arm.

"Baby, talk to me."

"Talk? Like what I've been trying to do since the day you walked out on me?"

"Do you not understand how hard it is to know that she's his child?" I said with a tear falling from my eye.

"Wes, you told me that no matter what you were going to be there for her and I. You said no matter what, she was your child. I didn't force you to say that. I'm just upset that you couldn't be a man of your word. You knew what the possibilities were when you got into this. I have not slept with Mike since the day I left him. You walking out on me made me feel like in some way I betrayed you and that's fucked up. By the way, her name is Whitney Wiley," she said before slamming the fridge door and walking away from me.

She was right. I did tell her no matter what we were going to make it through the end together, and I let her down. I painted this picture-perfect scenario when I may not be ready to be a step dad. Being a step dad isn't the part I'm worried about. The idea of having to deal with Mike for 18 years makes the hairs on my back stand up.

I wasn't going to run after her and beg her to talk to me. I assume she's tired and need some rest. I sat in Whitney's room in her rocking chair watching her sleep. She looked so peaceful. She has a brown complexion, a mole on her cheek, and short curly hair all over her head. She was beautiful. At this moment, I realized she didn't choose to be brought into this fucked up situation. So why should she have to pay for the decisions we all made not considering her? I sat there and watched her sleep until I fell asleep right there in her rocking chair.

****

Mica

They both looked peaceful and flawless sleeping. Walking into Whitney room to see Wes sleep on the chair made me forgive him for everything he had done. The way he made me feel vanished and my heart is now filled with love and comfort. I didn't get to watch them sleep for long before he woke up and realized I had been watching.

"She's beautiful like her mother," he said.

"Isn't she?" I said, smiling.

I still can't believe she came from me. She's so perfect and precious. All the stress and bullshit I went through throughout my entire pregnancy, she could have had major health defects, yet she is perfect.

"Baby, I know I was in the wrong. At the time, everything was too much to process and I began panicking, thinking I would lose you and Whitney. I just don't want to lose you. You are still the woman I want to marry if you give me the honor of being my wife. We can take this day my day, step by step, but I am begging for your forgiveness," Wes said, barely breathing.

The way he looked me in my eyes and said all that melted my heart. If I didn't have to wait six weeks before I could have sex, I would have been on top of him quicker than a mouse on cheese. It's just something about him that makes me feel like a teenage girl again. The feeling I felt at 14 with Mike is the same feeling at 21 I was feeling with Wes. I was a fool in love with Mike. Many people told us we were young and wouldn't last. We proved them wrong; we lasted seven years. The feelings I have towards Wes makes me feel like we could last a lifetime.

****

Ashley

I've been calling Wes' phone since the day he fucked my brains out while thinking about his situation with ole girl. I have never felt more disgusting in my life. I knew he had a situation, but somehow, I thought we had this under control. I mean, we just got back in contact. I figured we'd have a couple weeks, maybe months, of sneaking around before this all would blow up in our faces. I never liked side bitches, but I would play the side for Wes; that's the kind of power that man has over me. That's the kind of power he has over any woman he has ever touched.

I'm supposed to be finishing up my mother's funeral details, but all I have on my mind is him. I can feel him still inside of me. I keep replaying that night in my head cause Wes and I never had rough sex that much. The way he was being rough that night made me want more. He could at least answer his phone and tell me he's alive. He has been ignoring my calls and texts. I was driving from the café when I see Wes' car. I parked, waited for him to come outside and followed him all the way home. Now that I know where he lives, I will eventually make him speak to me again.

****

Mica

I was now adjusting into this new mother phase in my life. I am breastfeeding Whitney, and she has a good sleeping pattern already. She barely gets up in the middle of the night and when she does, she just wants a bottle and goes right back to sleep. She's a great child. Wes was out handling some business. I guess some west side niggas been trying takeover his blocks. Although I wish he didn't leave, I know that with having a child, the money must maintain.

I ain't seen Jas since the shit that happened with Nyla, and I was missing my friend. She had reached out to me a couple of times, but I kept ignoring and avoiding her because the hurt I felt that night seeing her down talk me cut me so deep. I felt that shit in my chest. Being friends since the 3rd grade, we shouldn't let this little shit come between us. Wes said she's been begging to see Whitney since I gave birth, but out of respect for me and my wishes, he told her to wait till I reached out.

Ring Ring

She picked up on the second ring. "Bitchhhhhhhh!"

We both started laughing. It's amazing how bonds work. I was so mad at her and all she had to do was say bitch in a goofy way and everything else was forgotten.

"I've missed, you best friend," I said with a smile on my face.

"I missed you too. You at the crib? I'm in the neighborhood, I'm about to pull up."

"Okay," I said.

I looked at Whitney, grabbed her hands and started moving them around. "Auntie coming over, auntie coming over."

She was smiling and giving me her little adorable laughs. I put her in a play pen and tried to straighten up a little before Jas made it over. We have a lot to catch up on, including how come she has never told me she liked pussy. We been friends forever, I expected to be the first person to know.

****

Jas

I'm overwhelmed with joy because Mica called me. I ain't waste no time pulling up on her and my niece. Mica nor Wes sent me any pictures of her, and I can already imagine how beautiful she is. I already know Wes not the father because he told me, but knowing what type of man my brother is, he is still going to treat her as if she was his own.

As soon as I pulled into their driveway, I parked my car, hopped out without locking my doors and started banging on theirs. Mica opened the door looking so flawless as if she never even had a child. She has always been eye candy for anybody who looked at her. She was that beautiful.

We didn't say Hi to one another. We literally stared at each other for a good 30 seconds and started hugging. I didn't want to let her go. My friend of 13 years had just went through labor without me by her side. We promised one another years ago that we would experience all those things together.

"Where is she?" I said, breaking away from the hug.

Mica moved to the side and Whitney was there playing in her play pen. I covered my mouth and cried because of how beautiful she was. Regardless of how much a shit bag Mike is, evidently, he makes gorgeous babies.

"She is so adorable. Oh my God, Mica!"

"Thank you. Now let's catch up," Mica said, grabbing the blunt off the table in her hallway.

Mica and I always vibe over weed. Wes use to call us "Best Buds" because of how much weed we smoked together.

"Match that shit then bitch," I said, pulling the blunt I rolled before coming over out of my purse.

We talked for hours about everything we missed in one another's lives. She'd been busy being a step mother and preparing for her baby girl while dealing with all the drama with two niggas in her life. Myself, on the other end, I been keeping shit low after Nyla. I ain't been on no dates nor had any sexual attention since her. I'm scared of ever being put into a situation like that ever again. Wes and I still haven't talked about what was going on between Nyla and me. He ain't asked, and I ain't volunteered no details.

For the rest of the night, we smoked a couple more blunts while watching Whitney roll around in her play pen. Time began to move fast and before I knew it, I was knocked out on the couch with Mica's head laying on my lap.

Chapter 12

Wes

All day I been away from home and my babies dealing with some bullshit in the streets. Word of mouth is some out west niggas trying to close in on me and take something I worked hard for since a teenager. I'm with all the bullshit and play crazy for real, so I had to go handle that shit. I got my right-hand man, Trey keeping his ear to the streets and seeing what people talking about, so I can get these niggas before they try to get me. Trey a cool lil nigga. I've had him under my wing since he was 15. He reminded me so much of myself. He's 18 years old now. He got that grind and hunger in him I had as a kid. I can ask him to blow that bitch at anybody and he is doing it without questions. His loyalty to me and my work. That is why I consider him as the brother I never had.

I've been yearning to be back home under my woman and child all day. I ain't even feel comfortable leaving the house. I want all the extra time I got to spare spent with them. As well as making up for the time I missed while being unfaithful with Ashley. I have no intentions on telling Mica the truth. What she don't know won't hurt her. Especially if I'm trying my hardest to make up for it.

Wifey: Can you grab me something to eat? In return, I'll show you what this mouth do.

Shit like that is why I love that girl. She so funny and freaky. That text alone has my dick standing up, craving to feel her insides. She can't even have sex for six weeks but willing to put her mouth to work for the mean time. That girl a true team player.

I stopped at Harold's Chicken on 87th to get her favorite, wing and gizzard combo covered in mild sauce. I was walking back to my car when I saw Ashley get out of the car next to me. You would think she was following me with the look she had on her face.

"Hey stranger," she said.

"Scanning," I said while unlocking my doors and trying to hop in. I didn't want to hold any conversations with her. I ain't want to speak on what happened between her and I. I was over the situation; it was a mistake and now a part of my past.

"SO, YOU GONE ACT LIKE YOU DONT KNOW ME?" She yelled before I could close my door.

I sat the food down on the passenger seat and got out.

"Look, you knew I had a girl and a baby on the way. You knew I wasn't leaving her. I told you that. I'm not acting like I don't know you. I'm acting like I wanna save my relationship and forget the other night even happened. I don't have feelings for you, Ashley. I am in love with Mica. The other night will never happen again for me and you. Now save yourself the embarrassment and don't ever buck up on me like that again. Goodnight."

That's all that was needed to be said. She just needed to be put into her place. In a perfect world, I'll never see her again.

When I got home, I noticed Jas car was outside. What I walked into 8-9 months ago wouldn't bother me, but I was pissed. Jas and Mica were both sleep on the couch. Mica's head was laying on Jas lap. After the shit that Jas and Nyla pulled on me, I don't even trust my sister around her best friend of 13 years.

"Man, wake yawl ass up," I said, startling Whitney and she started to cry.

"Baby, what's wrong?" Mica said.

Jas just looked at me with a blank expression like she doesn't know what the problem is.

"Jas, it's time for you to go home, sis. We about to call it a night," I said, looking at her as if I could choke her. She got up kissed, Whitney on her forehead, said bye to Mica and Left.

"Baby, what was that about?" Mica asked

"The way her and Nyla got over on me was unacceptable. I don't trust her around no woman alone that I'm involved with."

"Understood, now do I smell Harold's chicken and gizzards with mild sauce?"

That woman knows her food. To be as petite as she is, she could eat anyone out of a house and home. We both laughed, and I handed her the bag.

"Eat up greedy," I said, taking Whitney from her arms.

You would think I've been starving her the way she was banging that food.

****

Mike

I told Sean about some of Wes' spots. Wes may run the southside, but Sean runs the west, and he ain't never been scared about crossing sides. I feel like the only way to get more of Mica's time is having him out in the streets chasing drama.

I met up with Sean to get details on what happened.

"Yo, that clown ass nigga so dumb. He got the young boy Trey looking into me when I got Trey looking into him," Sean said, laughing.

Everything sounded like it was going as planned,.I never met this Trey nigga, but I know Sean trust him. That's all that I needed to know.

"So, what shit looking like?" I asked

"I told them niggas on his blocks to move around. They act like they ain't hear me, so I'ma have to stand on these niggas necks," Sean said with a very certain expression.

"Aight, well good-looking fam. I'ma holla at you later," I said while shaking up with Sean and going to my car.

I rode pass one of the blocks Wes be on a lot. I peeped his car outside, so I went to their home to try to see Mica and my daughter. I didn't bother calling her and warning her for my visit because I'm aware that Mica likes action. The same way Wes swooped in and took her from me, I was going to swoop in and take her right back. I knocked on the door three times before she opened it.

She was looking edible. She literally looked like a mother. Her curly hair was up into a big bun with one strand hanging on the right side. She had grey sweats and a large tank top on, and house shoes. It was the most flawless I have ever seen her.

"Oh hey, how are you?" She asked.

"I'm good, just stopping by to check on you and Whitney."

"Well, she's taking a nap, but she wakes up every 20 mins wanting her bottle in her mouth. Would you like to wait for her to wake up?" Mica asked.

"Yes."

I walked inside the home, and it was beautiful. Last time I was here was when I was moving Cynthia's body out the basement. I can tell that the house decor was all Mica because of all the black and white I see. Black leather couches, black tables, white rugs, white lamps, black and white photos on the wall. Mica has loved black and white forever and always said she wanted her living room to be black and white. I took that away from her when we moved together on her 18th birthday. I picked red couches and she never had the desire to decorate after that. That's something that Wes has better than me; the capability to let her be her and express herself in the best way possible. I was too controlling. No wonder she ran away from me. I would have run away from me as well.

"She should be up in a few minutes. Want anything to drink?"

"No, I'm fine," I said.

"Well I'm dehydrated, so I'll be back," Mica said, walking into the kitchen.

Whitney was asleep in her play pin, looking pure as ever. We did a great job on creating her. Mica and I are both chocolate, so her complexion is the same as ours. Her curly hair is to die for. I was getting impatient waiting for her to wake up. I just wanted to hold her and see her for a while.

"Mike, come here!" Mica yelled from the kitchen.

I got up and did exactly as she asked.

"So, we are doing pop ups with no calls now?" She said.

"Nah, I was in the area and wanted to check up on yawl. I mean, if it's a problem I can go, baby," I said, sliding the word baby in so smooth.

"Mike, what is it you're trying to do? You wouldn't have come here if Wes was here. He's already afraid of losing me to you because Whitney is your daughter. I just want to make sure you have good intentions on being around," she said, staring me down like a hawk.

"Baby, my intentions are as pure as it gets. I fucked up by losing you. I love you, I love that little girl sleeping in there, and yes, I would love to be a happy family. Every time I'm around you, I feel like a teenage boy again. I've been respecting your relationship as best as I can. If I didn't respect it, I would have your mouth on my dick and hope you'd suck it with everything you've got, then wait your turn. That's how you make me feel. One look at you, and I'm face deep in your pussy. I want your body right now. Like yesterday. I want a do over. I want to make up for all the wrong I've done and start over. I'm not asking you to leave that nigga. I'm asking you to be open to the idea. The ball in your court, baby. I move when you move, and don't play no plays without yo call."

I can tell what I said bothered her, but not in a way that she wants to stop. She started crossing her legs real tight and biting down on her lip. If she didn't just have a child, I would have shot my shot in the most disrespectful way possible. In his house, right on his countertops where he eats his food.

Chapter 13

Jas

Mica been on my mind since Wes came and kicked me out of their house. I've never considered anything with her. Let alone ever looked at her in that way. I have called Wes 6 times since that day and he has not picked up nor returned any of my calls. At this point, its fuck him. He jealous because his bitch wanted me. Wes been this way since we were kids. Something doesn't go his way and then he cuts me off, expecting me to talk on his time. I'm honestly sick of it. Mica is my only friend, and Wes pretty much the only family I got. And he is taking that away from me because of his emotions. I'm going to reach out to Mica and even flirt a little. If she takes the bait, that's his problem. I wasn't thinking about her in a sexual way until he opened that door. Now I want her just as bad as he does. It's been a good two months since I seen Mica. She should be healed from labor about now. So, I decided to give her a call.

"Hey Bitchhhhhhh!" She said, causing me to smile from ear to ear because that means she missed me as much as I missed her.

"Hey, so I know you may or not be able to do this, but you wanna ride with me to Indiana to see my mother's grave? I've been having her on my mind lately and need to talk to her. We could get a room for the night with two beds since my big head ass brother butt hurt," I said while laughing.

"Yeah, we can do that. When you tryna go?" Mica asked.

"Shit, tonight if we can. Then we could see the grave tomorrow before hopping back on the highway"

"Okay cool. I'll let Wes know."

"Aight, talk to you later."

Now was my shot. The hotel was going to have two beds, but we're only going to need one. When we got off the phone and 30 mins later I had a text from Mica saying she would be ready at 8, which was perfect. Fort Wayne, Indiana was a good 2 and a half hours away from us, so this 2-hour drive will give me time to warm her up and let her guard down. In a way, it's fucked up because I'm not interested in Mica sexually. At the same time, she got two niggas' going crazy over her, so I wanna see what that's about. I showered, shaved, and washed my hair. I packed my strap in my bag. I bought it back before Nyla went to jail for those theft charges, but we never had a chance to use it.

I went to the store and grabbed all types of fun things to play with: wine, whip cream, strawberries, rose petals, bubbles for bubble bath. I even bought us both a swim suit in case we get in the jacuzzi. I'm gonna lay it on her hard; she won't even see it coming.

I picked Mica up at 8pm exactly. I didn't bother going inside to get her. I texted her and told her I was outside. I was not in the mood to kiss Wes' ass at all. He been acting like a straight bitch lately.

"On my way, give me 10 mins," she replied.

Reading that made my pussy thump like a heartbeat. I looked up to their bedroom window, and I could see Mica getting stressed. She was standing there with her shirt off and must have been talking to Wes because her hands were moving. I slid my fingers in my pants and started moving them in a circular motion around my clit. Her breast were perfect. I started picturing myself licking her breast and her moaning telling me not to stop. I closed my eyes and drifted away. Ss soon as I heard the house door close, I came all over my fingers. Mica hopped in the car looking frustrated.

"You ready?" She asked.

I put the car and drive and got on the highway with a scandalous plan in mind.

****

Mica

Lately, all Wes and I do is argue about him fearing losing me. He even started going as far as accusing me of cheating on him. Now part of me believes he's the one cheating. I ain't did shit with nobody, except that kiss Mike and I shared a long time ago. Wes and his jealous ways need to stop; I can't handle all that pressure. When Jas called me about going to her mother's grave, I looked at it as a getaway. I needed to get away.

The ride to Indiana was quiet. She didn't ask why I had an attitude, and I was happy because I wasn't in the mood to give her an answer. We pulled up to the Sybaris Hotel. I've never seen anything more romantic. I look at Jas like *"Girl, what the fuck?"* Before I could say anything, she nipped it all in the bud.

"It's all that was available."

When we walked into the room, there was two beds like she promised. The room still looked romantic; the ceiling, and walls were all mirror. There was a huge jacuzzi, and an entire room outside with our own personal tub.

"Girl, this room the shit." Jas said.

"Imagine one of my niggas in here fucking me all over this room," she added.

She sounded like my best friend, so that lightened my mood knowing she's picturing niggas in her head instead of me, like Wes is thinking. We ordered food and started drinking shortly after. Jas had bought three bottles of wine here and some weed, so we got drunk and high.

I'm a light weight and small, so it doesn't take much to get me fucked up. We were dancing around the room and being touchy, but that was nothing new. Jas and I always danced together and touched on each other. But today, those touches feel different. When I was grinding on her, she started digging her fingers deep into my hips, pushing me against her to the point where it felt like she was using my ass to rub against her pussy.

I'm drunk at this point, but I still knew right from wrong. That's why I never understood people who blames their unfaithfulness on being intoxicated. I know very well what Jas is trying to do, but the way she's grabbing me, and kissing on my neck feels good. I haven't been touched in these ways in a long time.

"Jas, we can't do this," I said, trying to get her to stop.

"We can do whatever we want to," Jas responded.

"What about Wes?" I asked.

"I won't tell him. We are best friends just enjoying ourselves. We probably won't remember this later," she said while rubbing the outside of my leggings with her fingers.

"Fuck!" I said.

I opened my legs, giving her the access to do what she wants. She put her hands inside my leggings and started rubbing her fingers around my clit while kissing, breathing, and licking on my neck. She took her hands out my pants, and I gave her a frown. I didn't want her to stop. She started undressing me while looking me deep in my eyes. Once I was naked, she threw me on the bed, got on top of me and buried her face into my breast. She was licking my nipples nice and slow, swirling her tongue around my nipple rings. I lifted her shirt up, pulled one of her breast out and began sucking them just the way she was doing mine. Jas grabbed my neck, choked me and began to kiss me passionately. I took my hands and rubbed the outside of her shorts. I've never done this before but it all became so normal and felt right. She got off me, lifted my legs into the air and started blowing on my pussy. I moaned very loud and arched my back up. She then placed her tongue on my clit and started swirling her tongue around it, sucking on it after every few licks. I could have come right at that moment, but it felt too good, I didn't want it to stop. She stopped what she was doing.

"You can cum. Imma keep making you cum."

I exploded in her mouth. That was literally the biggest orgasm I've ever had. She lifted her head out of my pussy and said, "Come here."

I got on all fours and she kissed me, causing me to see what I taste like. I tasted great. I then decided I wanted to try to go down on her. She asked me if I was sure because I had never done this before, but after the orgasm she just gave me, she deserved it. She laid on her back and opened her legs. I did exactly what she did to me. She tasted so sweet, and her pussy was so pretty. After she came, she got up, went to grab her bag and went to the bathroom. When she came out the bathroom, she had a brown dildo strapped to her body. It was far from small, but it wasn't unbearable either. It was legit perfect.

Jas came back to the bed, put lube all over the dildo and told me to turn around. She inserted the dildo in from the back, and it felt better than I imagined it would. She was hitting all my spots.

"You like this shit don't you?" She asked.

"YESSSSSSSSSS!" I screamed.

Mike nor Wes have ever made me scream the way I was screaming at this moment. She grabbed my neck and kept pounding me harder and harder until I came all over the dildo. Within the first 5 minutes of her being inside me, I had come over 5 times. I stopped counting after 4. When we were done, we showered, and she gave me more head in the shower. Afterwards, I slept like a baby. I can't remember the last time I drooled in my sleep.

The next morning when I woke, Jas had bought donuts and coffee while I was sleeping. She fucked up by trying to kiss me. I barely remembered anything from the night before. Waking up undressed pretty much told me what had happened. I didn't kiss her back, and she frowned at me.

"What?" I asked.

"Nothing G, you good?"

"Why you are acting weird? Last night happened obviously, that don't mean we about to make a routine out of it, Jas. I'm with Wes, and I love him. I will never be with you or sneak around like you and Nyla did."

I must have hit a soft spot, because that infuriated her.

"You love him so much that you had my pussy in your mouth last night, huh?" She said before walking out the hotel room. She texted my phone and said she was going to her mother's grave alone because she didn't want to be around me now. She would pick me up when she's done. I didn't mind because I didn't want to be around her either. I can't believe we took things that far last night. Although I can't remember everything, the parts I do remember makes me want her again. Just one last time.

Chapter 14

Jas

I know I shouldn't be mad at Mica for not wanting me, but at the same time, the moment we shared last night will forever be unforgettable. Last night was better than every moment I've ever spent with Nyla or any man I have encountered. It sucks that I came alone to my mother's grave. This is my first time coming since she died four years ago. She died of a heart attack at the age of 45. Nothing has been the same since she died. Not even Wes and I; we were a lot closer before all of this. Now it feels as if I'm left alone even though I have a brother. Although I did fuck his ex/baby mother, we had a fucked-up vibe way before her and I. So, he can't blame me for how dysfunctional we are.

When I got back to the hotel room, Mica had our bags packed and ready to go. We packed the car up and rode in silence almost the entire way home.

"Please don't tell anyone about what happened last night," Mica said, breaking the silence.

I ignored her. She can tell me it didn't mean anything to her, but I know it did. I'm not going to tell anyone, but I am going to have her whenever I crave her. While she's with my brother or without him.

I dropped Mica off at home. She got out the car without saying one word to me. She was back home in her comfort zone with the man she claims she loves.

****

Wes

It was about 1 in the afternoon when Mica came back home. I can't lie, I did not want her to leave, but I can't be mad at her because of what Jas and Nyla did. Mica wasn't cut like that; she never been that kind of girl. While she was gone, I spent a lot of time with Whitney. In the short amount of time we were alone, I had already grown a bond with her. Not only that, I got a call today from the social worker saying that Karisma can come back home with me. Now I'll have all three of my girls in the house with me. I didn't bother to text Mica the good news because I wanted to tell her in person.

"Mommies' home," I said, bringing Whitney to the door to greet Mica.

"There's my babies... I missed you mommas," Mica said in her baby voice.

"So, babe, I have some good news. They said I can come pick Karisma up. I now have full custody of her."

"What? Omg! That's amazing, baby," Mica said, smiling.

That's the reason why I loved her. She has always been happy for me and supportive of the situation with my daughter. Karisma isn't hers, but she treats her as if she was. I couldn't ask for anything better. Now that she's healed from the pregnancy, it's time for us to plan the wedding like we wanted to do.

****

Mica

Coming home and seeing how Wes was with Whitney made me realize I might have just made the worst decision in my life. The last thing I want to do is break his heart when he's been nothing but good to me. The worst part of it all is I don't think Jas and I can continue to be friends. She crossed the line. Shit, I did too. I will never be able to look at her the same. When I think of Jas, I think of her head between my legs, and vice versa. She made me reach an orgasm Wes nor Mike could ever get to. But it remains the same, Wes is the love of my life, and I wouldn't replace him with anybody.

I showered and started to cook dinner. I am making Wes' favorite, steak, potatoes and cheesy broccoli. I'd just got done pealing the potatoes when my phone started ringing. Wes was in the living room playing with Whitney. My caller ID read "Maybe: Mike". iPhone's were really starting to piss me off. I deleted his number for a reason and they still reminding me. Maybe I should block his ass.

"Hello," I said with an attitude.

"So, you give birth to my baby then try to cut me out the picture, Mica?" He asked, sounding hurt.

It's not that I cut him out the picture, I just put my family first. I understand he wants to be in the picture, but he had that chance before he was beating my ass.

"Mike, it's not like that. I'm just taking care of home right now. When things go back to normal, I promise I'll let you see her."

"Yeah, that or I'ma take your ass to court. You can't keep me away from my daughter, Mica, not you or that nigga."

Click

I understand his frustration, but why bring Wes up? He hasn't seen Whitney because I haven't allowed him too. Wes isn't a big fan of him, but he's not in the business of keeping a father away from his child. If Mike ever made me drag my daughter into court for a custody battle, I'll never forgive him. He shouldn't even want to put his daughter through that, especially when we can figure everything out as adults. He always had bitch tendencies. That phone call reminded me why I left his soft ass.

Chapter 15

Ashley

I finally got a hold of my son Michael's father. I been hitting him up on Facebook, Instagram, and through mutual friends for weeks. He doesn't yet know that he has a son. Now that my son is two years old and will be three in two months, I think it's time he met his father. Mike and I been fuck buddy's for almost 6 and a half years. When him and his girl would fall out, he would fall deep inside my pussy. I didn't care that he had a girl. That's why karma hit my ass like a ton of bricks and made me a mother. I didn't feel the need to tell Mike about Mikehale because I honestly didn't want to be with him, and I knew all he would do is try to keep me in Chicago. I have a lot going for myself back in LA. I've became successful and made so many moves in the past two years in LA than I made spending my life here in the city.

I saw Mike walking out the store, so I got out of my car and started walking his way.

"Mike!" I hollered.

"Wassup," he responded.

Like he had never been in my guts, like I haven't let him fuck me in every way possible. I've been his dirty freak for years. We go two years and some change without seeing each other, and all I get is a *wassup*. Wassup with the niggas I happen to give the privilege of having my time trying to shit on me. First Wes, now this nigga Mike?

"What's up? What you want? I aint' got no money," he said with an attitude.

Yeah, I forgot to mention, he was paying me for sex. 400 every encounter and we were meeting damn near three times a week. I didn't have to work while fucking him. He was covering all expenses. I don't consider myself a prostitute because he was the only person I was doing it with. I remember the first time we met.

I was at Walmart, and it was the day before valentine's day. I was walking past the flowers and he stopped me and asked, "Which ones would make you smile?"

I pointed at the lily's. He said thank you, and I walked away. I didn't expect to ever see him again; he didn't leave much of an impression on me until I got to my car. Coincidently, he was parked right next to me, sitting inside is car. When I got to mine and popped my trunk to put all my groceries away, he got out and helped me.

"I didn't get your name, beautiful," he said.

"That's because I didn't give it or offer it," I said, still putting my bags in my trunk.

"Why the hostility, baby? I ain't send you here alone."

"What do you want, sir?" I said, turning around to face him.

At that moment, I realized just how fine he really was. I mean, he was beautiful. His dark skin was to die for, long dreads, and pearly white teeth. His lips were big and juicy. I would suck on them anyway. His face alone made me gain a soft spot for him.

"I'm sorry. I just don't understand why you're harassing me when I just helped you pick some flowers out for a lucky lady."

He then pulled the flowers from behind his back. "You are the lucky lady. Mind if I get your number or you can take mine? Whenever you have a chance, let me take you out and make you feel good."

"Damn, getting freaky already, huh?" I said, pushing my luck.

"I can make you feel good sexually, but I wasn't talking about that. I want to make you feel good without the sex, have you glowing, and keeping your spirits up."

He was a true smooth talker. Everything he said just rolled off the tongue so perfectly.

"773-908-4588," I said, hopping in my and driving away like he wasn't still standing there. He didn't even have his phone out to store my number, but I hoped like hell he remembered it.

I got two blocks up the street from Walmart when an unknown number called me.

"I see you like to be chased," he said

I smiled. I smiled hard because I do like it.

"I see you remembered the number. You called on time. I'm pulling up to my apartment complex. I'll text you the address. Come help me put these groceries away," I said before hanging up.

I waited in my car for only three minutes before he pulled up beside me. We took the groceries in the house, and I offered him something to drink. He asked for a glass of water.

"So, you're single?" I asked, cutting right to the chase.

"No, I am not. I have a woman; we been together about a year. I don't like beating around the bush, so I'm gone give it to you in the most gutta way possible, lil mama. My girl a virgin; she doesn't even suck dick, let alone let me play with that pussy. I respect her decision and, I'm not going to force her to. I will never leave my girl for you. Not today, not next year, not never. But I can

guarantee you many orgasms, a lot of fun, money and did I mention many orgasm's?" He said, leaving me shocked.

I literally just got asked to be a side bitch. He scooted closer to me and asked, "So what you say? you down or not?"

"Um..." is all I got out of my mouth before his hands was between my legs.

"This feels good doesn't it?"

I responded with a nod. "That's all I wanna do is make you feel good, and looking at the way you are living, I can tell the extra cash would help out. I will pay you $400 every time you let me fuck your brains out. You have to be available anytime I need you," he said while opening my panties and rubbing the inside of my pussy lips.

"mmm" slipped out of my mouth.

"See? Just enjoy it, baby."

He kept rubbing on my pussy until his hands were soaked. I can't believe I was letting him do this to me. I didn't even know his name, and he still didn't know mine. The worst part of it all is I didn't know his age either.

"How old are you?" I asked.

"19, now shut the fuck up and suck this dick," he said, standing up.

He pulled his pants down and shoved his big dick down my throat. He was very aggressive but in a sexy way. He could slap me in the middle of sex, and I wouldn't give a fuck. Everything about him turned me on. I'm stunned because a 19-year-old could make me feel this way. I was 26 years old, and most men my age couldn't do the things he could.

While sucking his dick, I kept stopping, begging him to fuck me, but he kept fucking my mouth. He was finally ready to cum for me.

"I'm about to cum," he said.

I took my mouth off his dick, and he pushed it dick right back inside of it.

"Bitch, catch this nut. Don't let nothing fall. Keep sucking it, keep sucking it," he demanded.

He came all in my mouth, and I swallowed every drop. He started putting his pants on.

"Don't beg me to fuck you. I will fuck you when I want to fuck you. Don't call or text my phone unless I hit you up."

He then took $700 out his pockets and dropped it on the couch.

"I'll pay you $400 every time I fuck you. That's $700 because that's probably the best head I have ever

gotten in my life," he said before walking straight out the door.

Most ain't shit niggas would fuck you, then pillow talk, sell dreams and a bunch of lies. He didn't do any of that. He kept it real and that turned me the fuck on.

I ran to the door before he could disappear.

"So, what's your name?" I asked.

"Mike," he said before getting in the car and pulling off, leaving me disregarded like empty condom wrappers on hotel room's floors.

"Mike, I'm not asking for any money from you. I just think we should catch up."

"There's nothing to catch up about, Ashley. Do you not remember what the fuck you did to me?"

Right before Mike and I stopped fucking around, I had just had an encounter with Wes sexually. His dick was a lot better than Mike's. Unfortunately, Wes burned me, gave me chlamydia and without knowing, I gave it to Mike. He gave it to his girl, and that's how she found out he was cheating. He cut me off, which I understand. I didn't know that I had it, and as soon as I found out, I went to get clean. That's when I found out I was pregnant and warned Wes that he gave it to me. I knew Wes wasn't the father because after we fucked, I got my period twice. We weren't fucking on the regular, just every blue moon.

Then I fucked around and back tracked to Mike, giving him the shit Wes gave to me. Good thing they don't know each other because the way Mike's temper is set up, he was so angry, I thought he would kill the entire city of Chicago.

"I'm sorry about that, Mike, but I really need to talk to you about some things."

"Yeah, you a sorry ass bitch alright," he said before getting in his car and pulling off, leaving me there like a bum begging for change.

Chapter 16

Mike

Jas called me the other day talking about there's something she wanna talk about with me. Jas ain't never fucked with me. We ain't never got along, so I have no idea what she could possibly want to talk about.

"Hey," she said, walking into my new apartment.

She had kind of a salty look on her face. A lot of people don't know that I Inherited over half a mil when my father died. My apartment is in downtown Chicago. You can see the entire city outside my apartment windows.

"Cut to the chase. Why you here?"

"You love Mica as much as I do. Something has been off about her, and I figured we could help each other try to figure it out," she said.

Jas was a bad ass bitch. She came over with an all-black dress that hugged her body like a condom, silver heels, and her hair was straightened. Jas is tall for a female; those long legs would make any man beg to taste her.

"Mica chose who she chose. I can't make that girl do nothing she don't wanna do. I just wanna be involved in my daughter's life, but your brother is making it hard for me to do so."

That's the truth. I love Mica with my whole heart, and now that she has my daughter, I love her even more. Although I love her, I can't make her want me. I'm trying to get rid of this nigga because without him in the picture, my chances of getting her back are bigger.

"Well, I was just coming by to let you know. We on the same page," Jas said before walking out the door.

Why would she want to help me get rid of her brother? Things are just not adding up.

****

Wes

Ashley been blowing my line up since I left her ass naked in that hotel room. She's been sending threatening texts about finding out who Mica is and telling her what happened. After everything Mica and I got going on, this is the worst time to try and expose me. Mica has been very forgiving about things, but I don't see her forgiving me for this. Especially since I was fucking Ashley while she was in the hospital.

The social worker called this morning. They are dropping Karisma off and she will finally be in Mica and I's custody. We're not married, but I know she would be a great step mother. I'm more excited for Karisma to meet her sister Whitney. Mica and I been taking care of Whitney and in between, decorating Karisma's room. Her favorite color is pink, so her room is pinked out.

I never even had a conversation with Karisma about her mother dying. She never knew Cynthia was her biological mother. All she knew as her mother was Nyla, and they are both dead. She's young, but she's able to comprehend death. She's smart as hell for her age.

"Baby, she will be here soon. Grab the balloons out the bedroom," Mica said excitedly.

That just made me smile; the fact that she was more excited than me about my daughter coming home.

When Karisma got to the house, she was so happy and in love with her bedroom. She was attached to Whitney as soon as she seen her, and she was also on Mica's hip. Having all my girls in the same house just warms my heart. Now that's all left to get done is marry the woman of my dreams, but of course before that, I'm going to have to talk to Mica about this shit that's going on with Ashley.

****

Ashley

Mike and Wes both still won't speak to me. I should have been back in LA days ago, but I'm not going to leave without answers. I understand Mike's point, but that shit was years ago. Now he has a son that's two years old that he knows nothing about. Wes is a piece of shit. I didn't ask him to climb into my pussy. I didn't ask him to step out on his girl. What he's not going to do is decide when to have me open, and when to leave me looking stupid. I did some investigating and found out where he lives. I've been watching him for days to see when he comes and goes. He's been in the crib a lot playing house with his bitch and kids. I just want to get even. I have dreams of ending up with Wes. I just want Mike to know his child, and I want to be with Wes. Sitting with him by the water and talking just made me feel good. I know deep down if his girl wasn't in the picture, he would want me. I must figure out the right time to get rid of her. I don't even know what she looks like, but I'm certain she doesn't have shit on me.

From the way he was fucking me, it was like she was on his mind in a disturbing way. Like she had hurt him; he shouldn't be with anyone that makes him feel pain.

It's 4 o'clock in the afternoon and I'm watching Wes leave his home. He kissed his girlfriend who was holding their newborn in her arms, then bent down and gave his daughter Karisma a kiss, got into his car and left. This was the perfect time to make my move.

I waited about 15 more minutes in the car in case he would turn around or forgot something at home. I walked to the door as I admired his house. This should be my house; its huge and its beautiful. Looking at the home just gave me more motivation to finish her.

Knock Knock

She came to the door, and her mouth dropped like she seen a ghost.

"Why are you here?"

"I just wanted to talk to you," I said, trying to sound genuine.

"About how you were fucking Mike while we were together? Your apology so overdue that I don't even want it anymore. I forgive you," she said.

I never knew what she looked like. Mike made sure we never crossed paths, but the fact that she knows who I am makes me want to play the part even more.

"I'm in town for a few days. Mike told me where you lived so I could apologize. I really just wanted to speak to you woman to woman, so you could understand I didn't know as much as you think I did," I said.

I knew all about her. I just never gave a fuck. I fake cried. I deserve an award for how good my acting skills are.

"Come in, girl. That shit old. I ain't mad at you."

Mica put the baby down for a nap and turned cartoons on for Karisma. She went into the kitchen and came back with a glass of wine and two wine glasses.

"Let's discuss how dumb Mike is?" She asked, holding the glasses up.

For two hours we talked about how her and I met Mike. She told me the terrible stories about him beating her and part of me gets happy knowing I dodged a bullet. She even talked to me about how much she loved Wes and how much of a good man he was to her. If only she knew the truth. To my surprise, Mica was nice and down to earth. I now understand why they were so in love with her.

Wes walked in the house and almost shitted his pants.

"Baby, this is Ashley. Ashley, this is my fiancé, Wes," she said, smiling.

"Hey, nice to meet you. I've heard a lot about you. She couldn't stop talking about you," I said, gassing the situation.

Wes didn't fold. He said hello and directed Karisma to get her pajamas ready for bed. He left Mica and I alone to say our goodbyes.

"You have a wonderful family, Mica. It was a breath of fresh air talking to you. I'll be here for a couple more weeks. We should get together for drinks," I said, locking in my future to destroy the beautiful life they are living.

"Yes, take down my number," she said.

I grabbed my phone out as Wes was entering the living room.

"It's 773-209-8363, just call me whenever you're free," Mica said.

We hugged, and she opened the door. I turned around to see Wes.

"It was a pleasure meeting you," I said before walking out, feeling like a million bucks. He is guaranteed to call me if he knew what was best for him.

Chapter 17

Mica

Ashley coming by the house was at first backwards and unexpected, but she turned out to be a cool chick. Mike is no longer my problem and after talking with her, I now realize he played the both of us. I was kind of anticipating her call to hang out again now that Jas and I aren't on good terms. It feels good to be able to have girl talk with someone.

Wes had been acting weird ever since Ashley left; like he had something to say but didn't know how to say it. The guilt of sleeping with Jas makes me not want to nag him. I don't want to upset him, especially after everything I've done.

"Baby, you ok?" I asked, trying to be a good future wife.

"Yeah babe, just a lot on my mind. Two niggas from my blocks got killed this week, and word on the street is some out west niggas behind all of this," he said.

I now understand why he seemed bother; niggas were out there playing with his money. Wes been running his shit lowkey for years. He always said he never wanted his shit to end with gunfire.

"Well, baby I'm sorry you been going through that. The kids are in bed... how about we do something nasty?" I said, kissing his neck.

We got up and went inside our bedroom incase Karisma would have gotten up for any reason. We didn't want her to walk in on us butt ass naked. Wes wasted no time peeling my clothes off my body. Besides Jas, I haven't had sex since I gave birth. It was well past my six weeks. I've been craving Wes' dick for forever now. We pretty much skipped the foreplay and got right to it. After we stripped one another naked, Wes spit on is dick, turned me around and shoved his fat dick deep inside my pussy. I came within the first 5 strokes. Something about that man and his dick just does something to my spirit.

"This yo dick baby. Take daddy dick, take daddy dick," he said.

That just made me throw this ass back harder on him. Wes grabbed me by my neck, pulled me closer to him and started fucking me harder. He was kissing and licking all over my shoulders.

"I'm about to bust baby!" He yelled.

Like always, he came all in my pussy. The warmness of his nut made me cum again at the same time with him.

****

Wes

I couldn't even focus while I was up in Mica. After seeing Ashley sitting on my couch, my head been fucked up. I doubt she said anything because she would have been dead fucking with Mica. I honestly don't think Ashley understand who she's fucking with. At times, Mica can become heartless. I'd hate for Ashley to end up like Cynthia. I just want to marry Mica and everyone to just let us be happy. All we been doing is fighting back and forth with each other and with people that want to make themselves relevant.

"Baby, can we push the wedding up? Like, to this next week?" I asked.

"I mean, that's kind of quick, baby."

"Don't you want to spend the rest of your life with me?" I asked, looking worried because of the possibility of her saying no.

"Yes, of course I do," she said, smiling.

"So, let's get married next week," I said.

Mica kissed me on my lips and said, "Okay."

She laid on my chest for about 45 mins before she was completely knocked out. Now that all my girls were asleep, it was time for me to go holla at Ashley face to face. That stunt she pulled earlier makes me regret her even more than I did before. The fact that she pulled that shit with my kids in the house makes me even more mad. I slid out of Mica's arms, covered her up and got dressed. I stopped in Karisma and Whitney's room just to make sure they were alright. They were both sleeping so peacefully. I didn't bother calling Ashley to tell her I was on my way. I'ma pop up on her how she popped up at my house. It's crazy that she's acting like this because we were not even on that. We did some catching up, but I never gave her the idea that I wanted to be with her.

I pulled up to the hotel about 10:30pm. I went straight inside and banged on Ashley's room door. After the 10th knock, she answered in a silk robe. It was clear I just woke her up out of her sleep. For the average nigga, she was looking fuckable. That's not what I came for. I need to know where her head at and why she pulled the stunt she pulled. I need answers.

"I don't appreciate you popping up at my crib," I said, breaking the silence.

"And I don't appreciate you fucking me, then ignoring me like I'm some type of hoe," Ashley responded.

She was starting to make me hate her. The way she moves make the hairs on my neck stand up.

"What we did was a mistake, Ashley. I was going through shit with my girl and took it out on you. I'm never going to leave, Mica. I don't want to be with you."

"I DON'T WANNA BE WITH YOU!" she said screaming and mocking me.

She was acting like a real-life nut case. She has no right to feel the way that she feels. We barely spent any time.

"Look, I don't know what you want from me for real but stop playing with Mica. She not a joke, and she not as innocent as you think she is. You are putting yourself in great danger trying to be funny. That's all I came here to say. Have a good day," I said before walking out the hotel room door.

I can't continue to hide this shit from, Mica. She doesn't deserve that shit; she been nothing but good woman to me. After leaving the hotel, I stopped by a couple of my blocks to see how they were holding up because after that shit with the west siders, money been moving slow. Trying to get married next week requires money because I know even though we are planning something small, Mica gone want to ball out.

I finally made it back home a little after midnight, and Mica and the girls were still asleep. I took a quick shower and laid back in bed. Mica must have been having a wet dream thinking about me because she was moaning and pulling on her clothes. So, I did what I do best. I put my head between her thighs and let her have her way with my face.

****

Mica

Jas head was between my legs while both hands were on my breast. She was making me cum round after round. I didn't want her to stop, it felt so good. She finally came up for air and started kissing the side of my thighs all the way down to my ankles.

"This my pussy?" She asked.

"Yesss!" I screamed.

"Say it!"

"This your pussy!" I said louder.

"Say my name!"

"Jas, this your pussy! Fuck, I'm about to cum!"

When I woke up, Wes head was between my legs with a blank expression. In my dream I was making love to Jas's face, but it was Wes. This isn't the way I wanted him to find out about what happened between her and I. I haven't even seen Jas since we took the trip, so it's a surprise to me that I'm having wet dreams about her.

"Fuck you mean, *'Jas this your pussy'*, he said, looking as if he could choke me to death.

"Baby, calm down. I didn't mean it."

"You meant it alright. You just came all in my mouth thinking about Jas," he said.

"When we went to Indiana to visit your mother's grave, Jas got me drunk and had her way with me," I said, being honest.

"You didn't want her to do it? She did it without your consent?" He asked for assurance.

"Nah baby. At the time I wanted her to do it. It had been a long time since we did anything sexually, and I was so horny I needed it. I instantly regretted it after it happened and told Jas that it will never happen again. We haven't even seen one another since that night," I said.

Wes just sat there speechless. He looked like he had more to say, but he didn't know where to start.

"I fucked Ashley after you gave birth and pulled that DNA shit," he said, crushing my heart into a million pieces.

"Why'd yawl act like yawl just met? She claimed she showed up because of Mike," I asked, curious and needing answers.

"Look baby, I don't know nothing about that. All I know is I felt some type of way, seen her at the store and the next thing, one thing led to another. When I came back and seen Mike at the hospital with you, that shit tore me up inside. Only way to let out my anger was through sex or killing a muthafucka. So, I went back to Ashley's room, and I fucked her hard. It was nothing passionate. I was thinking about you. In my mind, I was punishing you for hurting me. She realized I was picturing you and got mad. After that, I ain't seen her again. I wasn't picking up her texts or phone calls, and then she pops up over here. I went to her room a couple hours ago to let her know she need to fall back, but she doesn't wanna listen. She is acting like she in love with me or some shit," Mike expressed, damn near not breathing.

I can't be mad at him. I fucked Jas and kept that from him. All that matters is that we are being honest with one another now. Ashley got hers coming, and I promise its gone hit her like a ton of bricks. She is playing crazy with my relationship, but she gone find out real soon that I play crazy for real.

Chapter 18

Mica

The morning after Wes told me everything that happened between him and Ashley, and he found out what happened between Jas and I, it was kind of awkward. It felt like we both broke each other's heart but weren't willing to walk away. That's the definition of love. Granted it would have been better if our hearts could have stayed whole, but love is not a fairytale. It's more than what you see on social media and in movies. Love has ups and downs. You just have to choose the right person worth going through it all with.

Wes and I were getting the girls dressed so Jas could come get them, so we could go handle some business for this speedy wedding we're trying to have. I just told Wes about Jas and I last night, so I doubt he spoke to her about the situation. After the girls were dressed, Wes and I just sat with our phones out, taking pictures of them. Karisma is beautiful. Unlike both her mother's souls, she is innocent and pure. Whitney was the most perfect newborn. She didn't cry a lot except when she's hungry or needs her diaper changed. She barely woke us in the middle of the night. She was perfect, and she as well is beautiful and flawless despite the shitty situation surrounding her.

Jas made it at exactly 11:15 in the morning; she walked in the door like nothing had happened between her and I.

"Hey niecey pooh," Jas said, making baby noises at Whitney.

Jas has always been great with kids. She loved kids so much that when we were kids, I always thought she end up having a child at an early age. She loved playing with dolls and pretending to be a mother; I thought it was cute.

"Before yawl leave, we need to talk, sis," Wes said, ending the auntie moment.

"What's up?" She asked as if nothing happened.

"I know about what happened between you and Mica," he said. Jas looked at me as if I betrayed her in the worst way possible.

"It was just one night, and we were drunk, bro. It won't ever happen again, and I'm sorry, Mica. I noticed how distant you been with me since we got back. I don't wanna jeopardize our friendship for some bullshit. We been girls way too long for that," Jas said in the sincerest way.

"I just want you to understand, anybody that try to fuck on Mica is dead. Only reason you're still breathing is because you're my sister. I allowed you and Nyla to pull that bullshit. I won't tolerate it with Mica. She is my heart. I hope that you have enough respect for me to never let that shit happen again," Wes said, not blinking once.

We all came to an understanding that things got too far, but we are still a family. It sounded like Wes threatened Jas, but I'm quite sure that was a guarantee. I just pray things never have to get to that point.

****

Jas

I've been playing my role well. Don't get me wrong, I love Wes, but I want Mica. It took everything in me to not bend her over in front of him. His threats hold no weight with me. To be honest, I'm tired of him playing with me like I'm a joke and talking to me crazy. That has always been his problem; he always tried to treat me like a kid. It's becoming old and played out.

Mike still hasn't been able to see his daughter because of Wes. So, I made sure he knew I had her, so he could come over and bond with her for a little.

Mike showed up at my door 15 minutes after I sent him the address. He rushed to Whitney and picked her up. Karisma was in my bedroom watching cartoons. She came out to ask me to press play on the DVD and Mike instantly stopped like he had just seen a ghost.

"Whose child is she?" He asked.

"Wes and Nyla baby."

"She looks exactly like I did as a child. Nyla who?"

"Well, Cynthia gave birth to her, but Nyla raised her with Wes before she died," I said, confused by what he was saying.

"Cynthia and I use to fuck with each other while she was fucking with Wes."

"You're not saying what I think you're saying, right?" I asked. At this point, I do feel bad for my brother. Both these girls may not be his.

"You mind if I run and buy a DNA test? Please Jas. If she's my daughter, I deserve to know," he begged.

I let him go and get it. When he got back, he swabbed his and Karisma's mouth and put the q tips in a zip-lock bag. The instructions said he should have the results within a week. A week from today, Mica and Wes will be getting married, and I doubt Mike knows anything about that.

"You know they are getting married in a week?" I said while he was holding Whitney.

"No, they aren't."

"Yeah they...."

"NO, THEY ARE NOT, JAS!" He yelled, cutting me off.

The topic put him so on edge that he put Whitney down and walked out the door. I wonder what his next move is. Hopefully his next move is good enough that I won't have to make mine.

Chapter 19

Mike

The fact that Karisma looks exactly like I did as a child scares me. It's possible that I may have missed out on so much of her life already as her father if these results come back the way I know they will. Not only that, Mica is already about to marry this nigga. I gotta sneak to Jas crib just to see my daughter. Part of me wants to take Mica to court, but I know if I do that, nothing will ever be right between her and I. Only thing Mica must do to get the judge on her side is tell them how I use to lay hands on her. Better yet, how I pistol whipped her, and no judge will vote in my favor.

I've made many bad decisions as a boyfriend when I had her. I learned from them all when she walked out on me. In all honesty, if she would have stayed with me, I wouldn't have ever changed for her. They say you never know what you have until its gone, and I am seeing it first-hand now.

Mica hasn't answered any of my phone calls in a long time, so I shot her a text letting her know I needed to talk to her. It was worth a try.

Me: I need to talk with you about our daughter

She responded almost immediately.

Mica: Meet me at the house in an hour

I tried to plan out a perfect way to approach her, so she'd be on my side instead of shutting me out like she has been doing. I got to the house in exactly an hour. Like always, Mica looked stunning. She had her curly hair down; it looked like it had grown a lot. Her skin was as clear as ever, and she didn't have any makeup on at all. She was wearing dark blue jeans with cuts in the thighs, a black tank top, and black Jordan's. She was dressed so simple but could outshine anyone.

"Hey," she said with a smile on her face.

For a second, I felt as if she was happy to see me. She opened the door wider, so I could come in.

"Whitney isn't here. She's at Jas' house for the next two days while Wes and I plan our wedding," she said, blushing.

"Are you sure you want to do that, Mica? I mean, you and him just got together, baby girl. Part of me feels like you're not over me yet," I said.

She just looked at me with a blank expression. I know I planned to have more of a humble approach, but I'm tired of beating around the bush.

"I'm happy," she said.

"You're not happy, Mica. You're comfortable. You're in love with the thought of having a family," I said, bursting her bubble. "I'm not here to tell you how to live your life, Mica. I just want you to understand that you nor Wes will force me to surrender and exit my daughter's life. She's just as much of my daughter as yours, and if we have to go through the courts then so be it," I said.

"This makes you uncomfortable, huh?" She asked. She then walked closer to me and put her arms around my neck. "You want me all to yourself, don't you?" She asked me while bringing her lips closer to me. "You miss all of this. You miss the way I feel, the way I taste, the way I treated you. The sad part is, you missed your beat, Mike. I will always love you, but I belong to Wes. I could fuck you today and still wouldn't leave him for you. You just need to get used to the idea of another man being in my life that isn't you."

She was teasing me; how close she was to me made my dick get rock hard. Mica always knew she had me wrapped around her fingers regardless of whatever we have been through. I grabbed her by her hips and pulled her closer to me.

"You don't miss this? The idea of having two men in love with you turns you on, don't it? The fact that he won't leave, and I won't leave, gets your pussy wet, Mica. Admit that you want me to bend you over on this couch and fuck you hard, so you can shower, make him dinner, and pretend nothing ever happened," I said, pressing my lips against hers.

I figured she would pull away or tell me to stop, but she kept letting me kiss her. She bit down on my lips, which told me she wanted me just as bad as I wanted her.

"Admit it," I said, grabbing her by her neck.

"I do. but we can't do this Mi-"

I cut her off and threw her on the couch. "Take those jeans off right now," I said.

She did exactly as she was told. I got down on my knees and began to eat her pussy on the couch that he probably watches his games at.

"Shit," slipped out of her mouth as I placed my tongue on her clit.

I made love to her pussy with my mouth. She was so wet to the point it was tripping down her legs. I inserted two fingers inside of her while still licking her clit with my tongue.

"Faster," she begged.

I did as I was told and started digging and licking faster. After a few thrusts, she came all over my face. "Turn the fuck over," I demanded.

I pushed my dick inside her with no condom once again. It felt as if I had never left it. Her pussy wrapped my dick like a glove. I was only inside her for two minutes before she started creaming all over my dick. Every time I went deeper inside her, she screamed.

"You like this?" I asked. She didn't respond and just kept moaning. I smacked her on her ass hard. "YOU LIKE THIS SHIT?" I asked her again.

"Yesss Mike."

"Tell me, tell me you love this dick."

"I love this dick."

I started fucking her harder. I pulled out and made her sit on my dick. She got on both her feet and took the lead. She was bouncing up and down my dick like it was the last time she may ever get another good nut.

"Cum all on my dick," I said, grinding harder inside of her,

"I'm summing!" She screamed.

I pulled out and came all over her ass, stopping her nut. Mica turned around like I just committed murder, or like she would murder me.

"What the fuck, Mike?"

"You're about to be a married woman, get your nut from your husband," I said before putting my pants back on and walking out the door. Mica was yelling some shit, but I smiled and ignored her. She not ready to be married. If I could have my way with her the way I just did, I'm far from out the picture.

****

Mica

I can't believe Mike just did that shit. I can't believe I did that shit. I just fucked Mike, Wes and I just made up, and here I am being unfaithful again. I can't explain or say anything to justify my actions, but Mike has this hold on me sexually. Emotionally, I have no feelings for him, but every time I am around him, he turns me on. I could fuck him at a bus stop if that's where I seen him. It doesn't matter where we are, he gets me hot and ready. In this case, it just happened to be the house Wes bought me. I admitted and told the truth about what happened between Jas and I, but this is something I'll take to my grave before telling Wes. He forgave me for the shit with his sister. He would never forgive me for this. At least Mike didn't nut inside of me; he came all over my ass.

After he left, I went in the shower and finished myself off. I kept trying to get my mind to focus and think about Wes, but it kept drifting off to Mike. The way he moves, and his aggressiveness always made me go crazy. Part of me will always love Mike, but I know the smart move is Wes. Not that Wes is an insurance policy or anything. I love him deeply, it's just tough to throw away the seven years I spent with Mike like it never happened.

When I got out the shower, I got dressed to meet Wes for dinner. After today, we are both getting hotel rooms until we get married. He had this plan of us not seeing one another because it would make us crave each other more. We met in downtown Chicago at Catch 35 for dinner. The restaurant reminds me of reality shows. It was very classy and expensive. I told Wes I would be happy with Harold's on 87th, but he insisted on coming here.

I wore a red Dolce & Gabbana dress that hugged my body like a glove, and black Saint Laurent heels. I never put heat to my hair, but I straightened it for this occasion and had all silver accessories on.

Great minds must think alike because Wes was wearing a red Dolce & Gabbana blazer with all black slacks, and all black Jimmy Choo's. He was looking fly. That's one thing I love about that man; he always matches my fly, no matter the occasion.

As I was walking to our table, Wes got up, greeted me with a hug and told me I was beautiful before pulling my chair out so I could sit down. Being from the projects, and everything him and I both have endured in love versus where we are now, is breathtaking. We deserve this moment. We deserve to ball out; we've worked for it.

Wes always amazes me. When I got to the table, they were already bringing our food to us. He ordered me Florida Shrimp Scampi covered in butter, garlic, wine, tomatoes, goat cheese, and chives; it looked delicious. He even had me a glass of my favorite wine Summer Days sitting next to me. He ordered himself a Classic Steakhouse Burger covered in cheddar cheese, lettuce, tomato, onion, and mayo.

He had really out did himself tonight. Every time I get around Mike, he makes everything in my mind disappear because his sex is good. When I get around Wes, every reason for why he is the man for me hits me like a ton of bricks. His good outweighs his bad, versus Mike who can't give me anything good besides sex.

Wes and I talked and laughed about everything we did to get to where we are now. We even reminisced on old memories from when we were kids. This is a proud moment. After all the bullshit, we are about to be married, and spend the rest of our lives together raising our daughter's. This is the life.

After dinner, we went our separate ways to our hotels. He chose a hotel on the opposite side of Chicago; I chose mine downtown. We agreed no phone calls, only texts; we also said no masturbation. When we finally get in front of one another, that going to be one hell of a nut.

Chapter 20

Wes

Wedding Bells

Today is the day I'm going to marry the woman of my dreams. I've waited for this moment since I was in the 5th grade. The time has finally come. I wish my mother was alive to witness this moment. The truth is, Mica and I both come from broken families. This wedding will consist of our friends, the little family we have, our daughters and my sister Jas.

I have 10 hours to prepare for this wedding and see my beautiful wife walk down the aisle. I know she's going to look magnificent, she always does.

I called Jas and told her to bring the girls to me. I wanted them to ride with me to the wedding. The last few days planning all of this has had me so busy that I haven't gotten a chance to sit down and think at all. Now that I have that chance, only things floating in my head are thoughts of my wife and daughters.

When Jas dropped them off to my hotel room, they both were in white and pink dresses with hair bows in their head. Karisma ran into my arms.

"Daddy," she said, smiling.

This is a perfect example of what I want to come home to everyday for the rest of my life.

****

Ashley

So, I heard from a little birdy that today was the day Wes and Mica would be getting married. She hasn't even noticed that she checked into the same hotel as me. She even set up arrangements to have a driver to drive her around. Little did she know, that driver would be me, and she'll never make it to her own wedding.

I sat in the black Benz with the tinted windows waiting for her to come outside. I had my hair pulled back into a sleek pony tail, and wore a black dress shirt, and dress pants. There was no way she would realize who I was because I didn't plan to speak to her, just drive her where she needed to go. Right when it's time to go to the wedding hall, miss perfect life will disappear. I have a mean ass English accent, so if she did decide to speak to me, she still wouldn't notice. I've learned so many languages in college, I could pretend to be an Asian.

Mica hopped in the car. "Take me to the nearest beauty supply store; I need to get some lashes," Mica said without saying hello, or introducing herself. She is a rude stuck up bitch. That's more reason why in my eyes she doesn't deserve a man like Wes. Hell, she barely deserved Mike even with him beating her ass. Her attitude is nasty. She has to be putting a front on for Wes because he wouldn't tolerate shit like this.

After I took her to the beauty supply store, we stopped by the place she purchased her dress, and grabbed it, then she gave me the address to the hall. Mica was too busy in her phone, probably taking pictures for snapchat like most these young girls that she didn't even notice I was going in the opposite direction then the hall. After 30 mins of driving, I pulled up to a trailer home my mother had purchased when I was a kid. I took my 9mm out and pointed it at her

"You're not marrying my man, bitch."

****

Mike

The last encounter I had with Mica, I thought maybe she would reconsider this fairytale about marrying Wes, but she didn't. Today I got the DNA results on Karisma and just like I guessed, she was my daughter. I cannot just let Mica run off, marry him and raise my kids like they are his. I parked two blocks up from the hotel Wes was staying in; I find out from Jas. I knew he would be passing this direction because it's the way he has to go to get to the hall.

I had a plan that would get him out Mica and I's life for forever. It should be me marrying her. After seven years, I'm supposed to just let her marry another man? I won't allow it. When I saw Wes' car coming down the street, I slid into the left lane and followed him to the highway. He got tinted windows, so I could barely see him, but I knew it was his car because I studied the plates. Once he exited off the highway, he had to go down a road where there weren't many cars around. I sped up and bumped the back of his car. When he realized someone was trying to knock him off the road, he sped up. That was perfect. The faster he goes, the farther he will fly. I hit him one more time, sending his car flying in the air. I watched it flip 3 time before it started smoking. I than pulled off to go switch cars with Sean and get ready for their *wedding*. When shit hits the fan, saying I was at the wedding is the best alibi. Best part is Mica will need a shoulder to cry on and that shoulder will be mine. I said I will get her back by any means. Although it took me longer than I would have liked, it happened. Fuck a wedding, this should be a funeral.

****

Jas

I told Mike where Wes' hotel room was because he expressed to me what his plans were. I gained his trust by keeping him in the loop of everything that was going on, even allowing him to spend time with his daughters. I knew he was going to flip Wes car over, and I also knew the girls would be in that car when he did it. I figured I'm killing three birds with one stone. Mike can get rid of Wes and the kids, and I'll tell Mica that Mike did it. She will never forgive him and BOOM there's me, ready to slide right into her life.

I got to the hall early enough to see the sad look on Mica's face when she realized Wes wasn't showing up. I sat down in the first row. An hour had past and there was no sign of Mica nor Wes. I've been stalking Mica since the day I slept with her lowkey. When I realized she was nowhere to be found, I figured I should track her phone. I sent her location to myself when she fell asleep at the hotel, and I've been knowing her every move since. Her location shows that she was at some trailer home. I grabbed my purse and left the hall. I drove only about a half hour before I pulled up to the trailer home. It was gross. It's supposed to be white but it looks brown, there was shit all over the place, and the outside needed a lot of work. I grabbed my gun out my glove compartment and slowly entered the disgusting home. There was no one there. I kept walking to the back room and Mica was tied up to a chair with a sock stuffed in her mouth. I ran to her and started breaking her loose from the hostage. As soon as the tape was off her mouth, she yelled.

"It was that stupid bitch, Ashley!"

I didn't bother trying to get details. I just needed her to get to this wedding, so she can witness my award-winning game plan to destroy her life all because I want her. The entire drive back to the hall, Mica just kept talking about how she's going to kill Ashley. She even complained a little about how she's going to have to shower and redo her hair and makeup. I just agreed to everything she was saying, trying to be the best, best friend possible.

When we got to the hall, Mica ran into her dressing room to get ready. An hour later, I heard a scream from her room.

"NOOOOOOOOOOO!" She was screaming, holding the phone to her ear.

****

Mike

I saw Jas running to Mica's room because she was screaming. I figured she got the call about Wes. After waiting 5 minutes for Jas to come out of Mica's room, I decided to go see what was going on. Jas was holding Mica and even faked her tears to seem emotionally involved in the situation even though she helped me set it all up.

I walked into the room. "What happened?" I asked.

Jas just looked up at me with a smirk on her face while Mica was laying on her chest.

"Wes was in a car accident. The girls were in the car with him. They are all in critical condition."

My plan to end him caused me to put my own daughter's in danger. Mica will never forgive me. I have no chance of winning her heart back. I wanted to destroy her relationship, not destroy her life.